SECOND CHANCE WITH THE PLAYBOY

At thirty, Annabel Simpson is the youngest doctor to take charge of a ward in the history of Oakwood Hospital. A possible closure threatens her position and spurs her into action. Organizing a charity bike ride from Brighton to Land's End seems like a good idea — until she is paired with her wayward ex, Marcus Chapman. But Marcus has changed, still grieving the loss of his daughter, and is determined to break down the barriers Annabel has erected. Can they find the courage to mend their broken hearts?

CHARLOTTE McFALL

◆

SECOND CHANCE WITH THE PLAYBOY

Complete and Unabridged

LINFORD
Leicester

First published in Great Britain in 2017

First Linford Edition
published 2019

A catalogue record for this book is available
from the British Library.

ISBN 978–1–4448–4166–4

Published by
F. A. Thorpe (Publishing)
Anstey, Leicestershire

Set by Words & Graphics Ltd.
Anstey, Leicestershire
Printed and bound in Great Britain by
T. J. International Ltd., Padstow, Cornwall

This book is printed on acid-free paper

Dedication

To the heroes and heroines
of the real Brighton to Land's End
motorbike run.

1

'What the hell do you mean you're shutting the children's ward down? No, this is some sort of joke, it has to be!' Annabel leaned forward, almost tipping over on her swivel chair. 'You can't send sick children on a ninety-mile trip for treatment!'

'I assure you, it is no joke. The hospital simply doesn't have the money to keep it open. We have to cut costs.'

Mr. Wild's slimy voice grated on Annabel's nerves. 'Is that what it is, Mr. Wild, a bloody cost-cutting exercise?' she spat, banging her hand down on her desk. 'No, it is a cost-cutting exercise that is tantamount to a death sentence for some of the children.' *Where did they get their ideas?* 'Look, Mr. Wild, you've told me. Now get the hell out of my office. Be warned, this ward will not be closing.'

'I think, perhaps, you need to look for another position, don't you?' His parting comment was clearly an undisguised threat. As he walked out of the door, Mr. Wild glared at her with his beady little eyes, reminding her of a sneaky, twitchy rat. The door slammed shut.

Leaning back on her chair, Annabel tried to think of something. There had to be another way. She pulled her long black hair into a tight ponytail. There just had to be something she could do to raise the cash to keep the ward open. It had already been an extremely difficult shift on the children's ward. Losing a patient was never easy, especially when it was a child.

A tear fell onto Annabel's desk as she thought about the child they just lost. Jasmine had lived on the ward for nearly two years as she bravely fought cancer, going home only at Christmas time and her tenth birthday. Each time, she returned a few days later. Even through all her suffering, Jasmine always had a bright smile for everyone, nurses and children alike. She would sit on another child's bed and read the little ones stories or just talk to the older ones. Annabel had lost count of how many times Jasmine's leukemia had gone into remission only to return a few months later. Today, her precious little patient would sleep forever, but just like the flower, her spirit would live on in them all.

Annabel tried to tell herself Jasmine wouldn't be in pain anymore, but that simple thought didn't take away the intense pain. She, like many of the other doctors and nurses, became emotionally attached to all their young patients. Oh, she knew she should keep her distance, but they were all so young and helpless. These children were the future. It was her job to make them better, to give them all a chance at life. She had failed Jasmine, and for that, Annabel would never forgive herself.

The ward closures were all because of hospital privatization. She knew that; Marcus would have said it was progress. But surely progress for progress's sake was a bad thing when it would come at such a huge cost? The thought of Marcus made her stomach lurch. She had tried to put any thoughts of him to the back of her mind. She winced as the memories came flooding back. For an entire summer, Annabel had followed Marcus around hoping that he would just notice her.

There wasn't a day that went by when she didn't cringe at the memories of her embarrassing behavior toward Marcus. Just because he had gorgeous blue-gray eyes and a body to die for didn't mean she had to act like an idiot. It was a painful memory and one she wanted to put back in its little box.

That was years ago. Now she was a qualified doctor, and how the years had changed her from the girl she used to be. So young and carefree, up for a laugh with the best of them, but now Annabel knew there wasn't time for men in her life. There was no way she was going to repeat the behavior of the past, and she was having an all-out job of keeping the children's ward open. Mr. Wild had tried several times to shut it down, but the nurses and doctors had beaten him. This looked like the ward's last swan song.

Grabbing the phone again, she made a quick call. 'Can I speak to Thomas Underwood, please . . . ?' Annabel waited. 'Yes, please tell him it's Doctor Simpson from Oakwood Hospital.' If there was one thing Annabel hated, it was jobsworth secretaries. She waited for the 'He's not in the office right now,' even though they would be sitting behind their desks playing with their stress-reliever snooker tables. She hid her surprise when she actually had Mr. Underwood get on the line.

'Mr. Underwood, I have just had Mr. Wild in my office saying the children's ward is shutting as there is no money left,' Annabel stated.

After ten minutes, she put the phone

down. She now had a slightly better understanding of the situation, but proving that any theft had been going on was going to be very difficult. She did some paperwork, but then an idea came at her totally out of the blue. One which might just save the ward.

'Rach, can you come to my office quick, please?' A small smile crept onto her face when she put the phone down this time. It was amazing that one small thought could spark off a brilliant idea — or at least it would be, if she could pull it off.

The door to her office flung open, and a disheveled-looking doctor stood in the doorway. 'Hey, boss, what's up?'

'That was quick, Rach. Been in the store cupboard again?' Annabel laughingly asked her friend. The look on Rachel's face was priceless. 'You're meant to be helping the kids, not administering to Doctor Walker.' She would have to speak to Rach about it at some point; they couldn't carry on their relationship at work. They had jobs to do, and fraternizing with a doctor from Accident and Emergency wasn't part of the job description.

'Do you still have links to all those biker groups?'

'Yes, my brother still rides with a group. What do you need?'

Annabel breathed heavily. 'The administrator is shutting down the children's ward. Apparently, there's no money to keep it open.'

'No, they can't! They need to stay here.' Rachel stammered as her face turned a beet-red color. 'But . . . but . . . '

Annabel held her hand up to stop Rachel from saying anything. She felt the same as her friend, but she needed to stay calm, or else she wouldn't be able to think.

'What do you think of a charity bike ride? Each doctor in this hospital as a passenger on a bike.' Annabel twirled her auburn hair around in her fingers. 'We could try and get local businesses to sponsor us. I was thinking a ride from Brighton to Land's End. I will put the children's plight out on Big City Radio.'

Rachel gave her a mock salute. 'I'm on it, boss. Give me ten minutes. All the bikers in Sussex won't say no.'

That was one thing about bikers not many people knew; they might ride huge pieces of metal, be into heavy music, and have long hair, but none of them could resist helping animals and children. Annabel hated motorbikes, always had since her friend had nearly died coming off one on a quiet country road. How he had been found so late at night had been a miracle, and it was that one incident which had spurred her on to be a doctor. When Rachel left her, Annabel phoned the radio station to get them to do a piece on it. The more people she could get involved the better.

The hospital loudspeaker rang out. 'Code Blue. Floor 3, room 6.'

Annabel jumped from her chair, sending it flying toward the wall. The office door didn't fare much better; grabbing the handle, she opened it with the force of Zeus. Adrenaline rushed through her body as she ran down the corridor to the room. Tracy was in trouble; she had had major heart surgery. *I'm not going to lose another child.*

When Annabel arrived, there were already nurses and two other doctors trying to resuscitate the young child. 'Get me the defibrillator,' Annabel ordered. The heart monitor remained flat lining.

'Chest compressions, come on! Do I really need to do your jobs for you?' Annabel's anger rose with each second that went by. Was that a blip? The flat line drew across the screen.

'Sorry, Doctor.' The mumbled apology went largely unheard as they continued to work.

'Fifty joules. Come on, Tracy, fight! Seventy joules.' Annabel shocked the little girl again. 'I'm not losing two kids in one day.' All of a sudden, the heart monitor raced back into life. 'We got her.' Annabel sighed heavily. That was close. Any more shocks with the defibrillator and she would have had to call it.

'Nice job, everyone.' Annabel prided herself on being strict on the ward but fair. Her staff knew that outside of the hospital, she would laugh and joke around with the rest of them. 'Take five minutes, everyone; go grab yourself a drink. I will stay with Tracy.'

'I will stay with her,' one of the nurses piped up.

Annabel extended her thanks and walked slowly to the door. As everyone exited the room, Annabel turned and gave a last glance at the monitor. Tracy's heartbeat was as strong as it had been before. She would be okay, or at least she hoped she would be. *Well, I'm on call tonight in case anything happens.*

Two hours later, Annabel signed the last piece of paperwork. Grabbing her bag, she locked the office on her way out the door. She walked slowly down to the garage. Hearing heavy footsteps behind her, Annabel turned around. It was the hospital's administrator, Mr. Wild. 'I know what you are doing, Dr. Simpson. The board and I won't stand for this nonsense.'

'And what exactly am I doing?'

'Just remember who pays your wages.'

'Is that a threat, Mr. Wild?' Annabel was incensed. What did he think he was doing?

'I don't threaten.' With that, he walked away and climbed into his brand-new luxury car.

She could only dream about owning a car like that. She had once gone to a car showroom to have a look at a new car. A sleek black one with a bright red leather interior. Annabel had loved the scent of the brand-new leather; new cars seemed to have a special smell all of their own. All the buttons you needed on the steering wheel so there was no messing about, a built-in sat nav on the dash. It had everything she would ever need, but even with financing, she couldn't afford the payments. She knew that she would never spend that much money on something like that. She had so many other things to worry about like toys for her kids on the ward. Or just keeping up with the bills at home. Some people got all the luck, but others had to work hard for what they had.

So that's where all the money has gone, shiny new cars for the board members. Okay, so she couldn't prove it, but something wasn't right somewhere, and after the head of the board telling her earlier that there was no money to keep the ward open, Annabel was determined to find out.

She climbed into her old beat-up baby. There was no way she would ever replace her car. The petrol consumption on it was great, and they had been through so much together. Annabel suddenly laughed out loud; she was being sentimental about a car. Flicking the stereo on, she tuned into the Big City Radio channel.

'Listen up, folks. We have a major dilemma over at Oakwood Hospital. There are plans afoot to shut the children's ward. There is to be a fundraising charity bike ride. Get in touch by phone to us here at Big City Radio or email Dr. Simpson at Oakwood Hospital dot com for more details.'

Annabel listened as the DJ changed the subject and began rambling on about the traffic jams. No, she didn't have to call the radio straight away, but she couldn't risk the ward closing without fighting with everything she had.

★ ★ ★

Marcus Chapman sat in his corner office finishing off paperwork. The mountain never seemed to get smaller. He'd been at it for hours, and he still had a huge pile to get through. At least his client had just made a considerable amount of money thanks to him and his investment advice. 'Nothing like blowing your own trumpet is there,' Marcus mumbled to himself. The radio DJ prattled on about all the local news when he suddenly looked up and stared. 'Oakwood Hospital children's ward closure. Bikers needed.'

He flinched when he heard the hospital's name, immediately grabbing the picture on his desk. A young girl lay sprawled out on a bouncy castle, her blonde hair surrounding her like a halo. His beautiful, sleeping princess. He felt a stab in his heart. Marcus was grateful to the hospital for all they had tried to do to help save his daughter after her short illness. He hardly went home these days; instead, he reveled in the anonymity and impersonal service of hotels. Marcus was tired of all the sympathetic looks and comments from his friends and family and couldn't bear to be in the house he'd shared with his daughter. Too many memories.

His life had been so empty since Emily had gone. The light inside him had been extinguished. She had made him sensible, and now, he had gone partially back to his old womanizing ways.

There were only so many times you could hear the words, 'Sorry for your loss.' Yes, they were words of comfort, but they were often hollow. Well, if they knew what was good for them, they would leave him well alone.

'A bike ride? Doctors and bikers together as one,' repeated the DJ. That was something else he hadn't done for so long — donned his biker leathers. He missed the open road, the rush of adrenaline that riding his bike gave him. He could suggest that his company be the main sponsor, anonymously of course.

He liked the idea more and more; he could maybe join in. Marcus sighed heavily; no, he wasn't ready to face the world, not yet. *That isn't strictly true is it, Marcus? You pick women up in the hotel bar just for a bit of fun. So you have been out in the world.* He had made a lot of mistakes, but his beautiful little Emily had definitely been the best thing to happen to him. He had done well for himself. Marcus couldn't deny that he had led the playboy lifestyle and would have still. Having Emily had grounded him for the few short years she had been his.

Josie hadn't stayed around. She'd simply dumped Emily on him and disappeared. That was fine by him — they hadn't needed her. Marcus knew he should have been more careful, but never had he thought that his daughter was a mistake. For her memory, he couldn't let the hospital ward shut.

Marcus stood up and paced around the room. Could he do it? Could he get on the back of a bike again? He wasn't really ready for the outside world just yet, but he also knew he couldn't sit around and do nothing. Marcus poured himself a whiskey from the bar in his office. Swishing the brown liquid around in the glass, he raised the glass to his lips but paused. Would his leathers still fit after several years languishing in the back of his wardrobe?

Marcus put the glass down, picked up the phone, and called the radio station instead, pledging two million pounds for the fund. Perhaps other people would do the same. That amount of money from an individual should push other companies to do their part. Out of gratitude or guilt, he didn't care. The only thing he did care about was that the hospital shouldn't shut that ward.

'Annabel trained as a doctor. I wonder if she ever made the grade?' he said aloud.

'Did you want me, sir?' His ever-efficient secretary, Mrs. Windbourne, popped her head around the door.

'No, I was just talking to myself.' She had already put her coat on, ready to leave. 'You take yourself off home,

Mary. I will be fine on my own.'

'Night, sir.'

It was hard to think of Annabel. A family emergency had caused him to rush out of her house without saying goodbye. But then, she had never contacted him again; Marcus had no idea where she had gone or even where her family lived. *Okay, so I should have asked beforehand*, he chastised himself. Then she had gone, and he did what he generally did in those days — moved on.

Something had always been missing; he had never felt that true love that people had so often felt. Where you don't know what you would do without that special person in your life. 'Oh, to hell with this,' he said, tossing his coat over his shoulder. Work could wait. If his leathers weren't going to fit, he would need to get to the shopping center before it closed at eight.

The traffic had died down now, and it only took him twenty minutes to get home. Opening the heavy oak door, he walked slowly into his home. Mail was piled up behind the door. Marcus bent down, gathering the heaps of letters and throwing them on the side table. It was too quiet. All Emily's toys still lay strewn around the house. Dolls shoes littered the stairs, and little dresses were scattered in the fruit bowl.

The guilt rose up in his throat. He felt sick. He knew he should tidy up and make the house more suitable for visitors, but the truth was, Marcus couldn't be bothered. He didn't care. Taking the stairs two at a time, he went to the upper level and into his room. With a yank on the wardrobe door to open it, he then hunted for his biker leathers. They lay crumpled in the darkest corner of the wardrobe. Unwanted, unloved, just like him.

After stripping down to his boxers and socks, he eased the black leather trousers over his toned legs. He smiled at himself in the mirror, surprised they still fit. 'Saves me a shopping trip.' Marcus grabbed a carryall from the top of the wardrobe stuffing his leather jacket, boots, and trousers into it. His bright yellow helmet sat staring back at him like a cat on watch at midnight.

2

Annabel had spent her spare time over the past several weeks liaising with the biker groups, thanks in most part to Rachel's biker contacts. The Farmers Pub Lancing's car park was already packed. Annabel had been told this particular pub was used by a bike group for their meetings, and a lot of charity runs and other rides already set off from here. So she decided that if others were already using it as a starting point, she would too.

She stood clutching the list of doctors and nurses who would be teamed up with which biker and from which group. Seeing Rachel standing alone, Annabel walked quickly toward her. 'Hey, it's a great turn out, don't you think?'

Rachel pointed in the distance. 'Yes, look. Even the local TV crews have come. We will do all right I think. Mr. Wild will not be shutting our ward down anytime soon.'

Annabel caught Rachel looking her up and down 'What's up?'

'You don't seem much like a biker chick.' Rachel's comment stung.

'Well, I don't think I could get these hips into a pair of leathers, do you?' Annabel frowned. She had always been on the curvaceous side. She had child-bearing hips — that's what her mother used to say.

'Nothing will go wrong, Annabel. Stop worrying.'

'I hope not, Rachel.' Annabel wasn't sure if her plan would work. 'Hey, have you seen Lucas from pathology in his pink lycra shorts?'

Annabel smiled as she thought of the reception staff doing the run pushing a bed. That would be hard work. After all, it would take them days to complete the journey.

Her friend nodded and then burst into peals of laughter. 'You look tired.'

'Thanks.' Annabel shook her head. 'Between organizing this and doing double shifts at the hospital, I'm exhausted.'

Because of all the monetary cuts this year, the ride was vital. Annabel would need as many people as possible sponsoring the riders or taking part in order to raise the much-needed funds. She had spent weeks contacting all the motorbike groups in Sussex to ask if they would take part and/or have a passenger with them. Not many of the doctors had bikes, but they were all game to ride a speed machine. But not many of the nurses wanted to ride on the back of one, so they just chose a pushbike to do it instead. All that Lycra made her laugh. She was accustomed to seeing half of them in hospital scrubs, not multi-colored shorts and tops, which clung to the contours of their bodies.

Waving the papers around, she said, 'I best get this to the announcer.' With that, Annabel wandered off, in search of the only person with a megaphone. *These bikers definitely like being loud. There's no way I can raise my voice enough for everyone to hear me.*

'I'll walk with you,' Rachel called after her.

'Thanks for helping me with this, Rach. I appreciate it,' she stated.

They walked along in silence amongst the rows of shiny motorbikes. A rainbow of color lined the pub car park. It was the first year of the hospital's charity bike run, which she hoped would become an annual event.

She had never before got involved in the charity or team-leading events, preferring to sponsor people instead and stay in the shadows. Annabel hated the damn things, but as she stopped at one motorbike in particular, her heart skipped a beat. The gold lettering stood out like a neon sign on the Las Vegas strip. Annabel looked at it hard; confusion reigned over her, why now? Why did he have to show up here? No, he could have sold it on. Yes, that was it.

Marcus wasn't here. He wouldn't think of anyone other than himself, let alone come out on a sponsored bike ride.

A helmet hung on the handlebars. Lifting it off, she held it in her hands. But her hope was short lived when she took a closer look at the helmet. It was bright yellow with a skull design painted on it. No, there was no mistake. She needed to get away. Anywhere away from that black bike and its owner. The other side of the world would be preferable.

That bike belonged to Marcus Chapman. She hadn't seen him for several years, and quite frankly, didn't want to. But in the throng of doctors, nurses, and bikers, he was obscured from view.

'Anna, what's wrong?'

Annabel didn't miss the concern etched on her friend's face. 'Nothing, it doesn't matter.' She tried to brush away the sour lime feelings bubbling up inside her.

'Bikers make better drivers.' The

male voice stopped her in her tracks.

'Because bikers are more aware of their surroundings.' The words automatically flew out of her mouth.

3

'Aren't you going to say hello then, Annabel?' a smooth sexy voice asked.

Rachel had nudged her in the ribs; hearing his voice, she knew who had spoken to her.

Annabel turned slowly around, coming face to face with Marcus. What could she say? *Come on, Annabel. You don't usually have a problem talking.*

'How are you, sweets?'

For several seconds, Annabel stayed quiet and allowed herself to drink in the sight of him. Marcus was dressed head to foot in black leather, two white stripes down each sleeve of his jacket. He still looked as sexy and hot as she remembered. 'Fine. I, er, I, er, need to go.'

Marcus reached out, brushing her arm with his fingertips. 'Surely not. We

27

have a lot of catching up to do.'

'Er, no we don't,' Annabel hissed back.

Annabel turned and fled into the crowd. She didn't want to give Marcus any further chance to talk. Her face flushed with embarrassment, she let out several deep breaths trying to calm her shattered nerves. The memories of that summer flooded her mind. It was her own fault; Marcus would have had plenty of laughs with his friends when he told them all about his night with her. Marcus was a bad boy biker, her pet name for him, which sounded so stupid now. She even felt stupid for coming up with such a daft nickname.

⋆　⋆　⋆

Marcus stood sadly watching her go. Not the reception he had expected. *Come on, Marcus. What did you expect? You didn't know she would be here. After the history you two have, it should be no surprise.* 'Is she always like that? I'm Marcus, by the way,' he said, holding his hand out to Annabel's friend.

'Dr. Rachel Nelson. Yep, pretty much, at least she is lately.'

'We were old friends.' Marcus tried to keep his voice even, but he wavered. Not that it would look like that to an outsider.

'Right,' Rachel replied. 'I best go see where she got to. Nice to meet you, Marcus.'

Marcus stood, his feet rooted to the spot. He could still smell Annabel's fruity perfume, the same scent she had worn years before. It was like she was a deer caught in the headlights. This was a mistake; if he had known she would be here, he would never have come. She had made it clear she wanted nothing to do with him when she had never called him.

A loud crackle and then a voice boomed over the loudspeaker, interrupting his reverie. 'Could all riders and hospital staff please congregate by the pub entrance?'

A surge of people ambled over to the door, whilst awaiting further orders. He had to admit it was very well organized and extremely well represented. It showed just how much the children's ward mattered to people. It mattered to him too. The staff at Oakwood had done everything to save Emily when she had meningitis, but his angel had been taken away from him much too soon. Now it was his turn to give something back.

The loudspeaker sprang into life again. 'I am going to read a list of names. Each pair I call out, could you both come to the front so that you can go to your respective bikes. I would also like to thank the private sponsor who has donated two million pounds to the Save the Children's Ward Fund.' A huge roar went around the crowd followed by a thunderous applause.

Marcus tried to keep his body language from giving the game away. He didn't need or want the publicity.

That wasn't why he had done it; Emily would have wanted him to help all the other little children.

The list of names was extensive, and each pairing went off and sat waiting patiently on the bikes. Annabel became increasingly nervous as fewer and fewer bikers were standing around. She had volunteered to be one of the pillion riders. 'Only two pairs left.'

'Dr. Rachel Nelson and Anthony Judge. The last pairing for the charity bike ride — Dr. Annabel Simpson and Marcus Chapman. All your bags will be following you in the van.'

Annabel's heart sank. The last thing she expected was to be paired with Marcus. *Okay, I'm a professional, and I can do this.* Annabel reluctantly walked up to the front and found herself face to face with Marcus.

'Looks like we're paired up together.'

'Looks like it unless this is a mirage.' There was a hard edge to her voice.

Marcus glanced around. 'No, it's definitely just us two.'

'Look, this is to help the hospital, but I don't want anything to do with you after,' Annabel replied. Did he have to look so hot? Her mind was troubled even more; the thought of having her arms around his waist again sent a shiver along her spine.

'That's just fine with me, and there is no need for the comment. I know what the ride is for.' *Great. This is going to be a good few days with the ice queen here.* Marcus couldn't believe he had just called Annabel that. He knew she was far from an ice queen. He sensed she had her guard up, not that he could blame her. Things hadn't ended the way he had hoped they would.

'Here, you need this.' Marcus handed her a crash helmet.

Annabel snatched the helmet out of his hand and put it on. He didn't need her to talk to tell him that she was still angry to have been paired with him. At least they wouldn't need to have any conversation until the first rest stop.

★ ★ ★

The little hairs stood on the back of her neck as she eyed the shiny metal suspiciously. She refused to admit that abject terror made her knees weak and a lump form in her throat at the idea of getting on the bike. What if they crashed? What if they got hit? She couldn't think properly as her body began to shake.

'What's this?' he asked, pulling the little backpack she carried.

Marcus brought her back to him. They were still in the car park and had gone nowhere. 'A few medical supplies. You never know when you may need them,' she replied.

'Oh, come on, Annabel. I'm a safe rider. Let it go in the van,' Marcus replied, exasperated.

'No, it comes with me, and those things aren't safe,' she said, pointing to his motorbike. She moved slightly away from him. *Doesn't he get it? Doctors always go prepared for an emergency!*

33

Marcus eyed her suspiciously before he answered, 'Just get on the damn bike.'

Annabel climbed on the bike first, sitting as far back as she could without falling backward. As Marcus climbed on in front of her, she couldn't help but notice how good his ass looked in a pair of leathers. *Come on, Annabel. You can't think like that. You need to keep your head on what we are doing and not eyeing up an old flame. Besides, he is totally besotted with himself.*

'Hold on tight,' Marcus demanded.

Following what he said, Annabel wrapped her arms tightly around his waist. The whole of her body reacted to his. Annabel's skin burned at his touch. Her stomach twisted into knots as she remembered the last time they had been this close.

As they set off, Marcus shouted behind him, 'Are you all right?'

'Yes!' Annabel screamed back.

The wind rushed past them as they weaved in and out of the traffic, diving to the front whenever there was a red light. This was the craziest and strangest thing Annabel had ever done. *It's only for the weekend; you can get along with Marcus for that long.* At least they wouldn't need to share a tent. *Please, please tell me he has brought his own?* Annabel needed to get off the bike and stretch her legs; surely, Marcus wouldn't make them go all the way to Land's End without stopping?

★ ★ ★

The other riders seemed to have outstripped them somewhere on the road. Marcus checked his mirrors. There were no bikes, and he couldn't see the van, but that could have been buried in the multitude of cars and lorries that were behind them. Spotting a sign for the next services, Marcus made the decision to pull in. Annabel and he needed to sort things out, and maybe they could catch up with the others if they had had the same idea.

Pulling into the services, Marcus headed for the spaces nearest the entrance so he would be able to keep an eye on his bike. 'Look, we need to talk,' he said, his voice muffled by the helmet.

'We don't have anything to say to each other.' Annabel folded her arms.

Removing his gloves and helmet, he said, 'I don't know about you, but I could really use a brew. Besides, there is something we need to clear the air about.'

'I guess a brew would be okay,' she conceded.

Marcus didn't say another word, just walked next to Annabel in total silence. There were so many things he wanted to talk to her about, and one he didn't. But it couldn't wait. He had to explain. 'Go sit down.'

He watched as Annabel sat on one of the orange plastic chairs. He loved the way she frowned when she took a look at the cracked Formica tabletop. He assumed that the large crack he could see from his current position wasn't the only one that littered its surface.

Marcus stood at the café counter, waiting to be served; he was busy rehearsing in his mind what he would say to put things right between them. He didn't really know what he had done. Annabel was the one who had never called. He had left his number scrawled on the takeaway box they had eaten from the night before. A voice interrupted his thoughts. 'Do you want anything?'

'Er. Yes. Two teas, please, love.' Why on earth did he have to sound like a total idiot?

The waitress placed the teas on the counter. Marcus handed her the correct money, and, taking a deep breath, he turned around. Time to face the music or the lightning strike, he wasn't sure what he was going to receive. He walked slowly but deliberately back to the table.

Placing the cup down in front of Annabel, he willed his hands not to

37

shake. 'Here, your tea.'

'Thanks.' A curt reply was all she gave him.

'Look, how come you never phoned?' Marcus asked, taking a sip of tea.

'I don't want to discuss it. We need to leave it at that.' Her ire had risen, judging by her tone.

Marcus could see he was pushing Annabel a bit too far, a change of tactic he thought and quick. 'Can we start again, Anna? Just be friends, maybe.' Did he sound too hopeful? Had his voice betrayed him?

★ ★ ★

Annabel thought for a moment. 'I guess we can try. Anything is better than being angry with each other all the time.' She held her hand out to him. 'Friends.' She still wouldn't forgive him for how embarrassed he had made her in the past.

When Marcus took her hand, she felt like she was back in the playground again. 'Why don't we stay and have something here? Wait for the rain to stop.'

'Good idea, riding with the rain blowing in your face isn't the best thing to do.'

Marcus grabbed a menu from the table next to them. He held it open between them so they could both see what they could order. It was the usual greasy-spoon fare; most things were served with chips and or beans. 'Nothing's jumping out at me.'

Annabel caught Marcus grinning. He was obviously thinking the same thing. 'We could have chips with an extra side of chips,' he answered.

They both laughed, lightening the atmosphere between them. 'I thought we could just go for chips.' Annabel felt a huge weight lifting from her shoulders. Perhaps this run wouldn't be so bad after all, especially if things could be like this between them all the time.

Marcus smiled, but it came out lopsided and made Annabel laugh even more. She had missed this. Here in the service station, she had no concerns. There were no patients she had to rush and see. It was hard to socialize when you were the head of a ward. Who would have thought that at only thirty she would head a ward when many doctors older than her still hadn't had that privilege?

'I think chips is a great choice,' Marcus replied.

'Well, we didn't have much to choose from,' conceded Annabel.

Marcus stood. 'I'll just go and order some.'

Annabel stared out of the window; the car park seemed to be getting busier. A lot of truckers had turned up. She presumed either to refuel or to take their mandatory breaks. If they planned to rush into the café, it was a good job they were just about to order. Her stomach twisted into knots each time she looked at him. Time hadn't dissipated her feelings, just hidden them away.

It wasn't long before Marcus returned. 'So what have you been doing with yourself?' she asked him as a sudden shyness washed over her. She felt like she was talking with a stranger, not someone she had once considered a friend and a lover.

'I own my own firm; I guess I have done well for myself.' He didn't like to brag, and generally, people would just befriend you for the amount of money you had or what they thought you could do for them.

'You ever get married, kids?'

'Er . . . no.'

She caught how Marcus had hesitated, but then Annabel thought that perhaps she was just prying too much. They hadn't seen each other in a while, and she had no real need to ask such personal questions. 'Sorry, I shouldn't have asked.'

'No, it's okay. I guess.' He turned away slightly as if he didn't want to answer any more probing questions. 'We're just getting to know each other

41

again.' He played with the teaspoon, twirling it around in his fingers. 'So what about you? Married, two point four kids?'

'No to both. I never have time for either.'

'I think you would make a great mum.'

She remembered Marcus used to like the way she blushed and nibbled on her bottom lip. It had always looked cute. The waitress came over and brought their plate of chips. They both thanked her and tucked into the British tradition.

'Why is it chips taste nicer by the seaside than anywhere else?'

Annabel laughed. 'I'm not sure I am up for such a demanding conversation.'

'Okay, I guess we can discuss the weather.'

'Running out of things to say?' She could tell he was just as nervous as he was. Surely they could have something to talk about. 'Do you still see Tommy?'

'Only when he is on leave. He joined

the Navy. Oh, do you remember Craig from the bowling alley?'

Annabel nodded. 'Yes.'

'Would you believe that he's a dad and a police officer?'

'No way! Mr. I-am-never-gonna-do-what-society-asks-me-to? That Craig?'

'Yes, I know, I couldn't believe it myself at first.' Their laughter filled the quiet of the room. 'How we've all grown from that summer.'

Annabel flinched; it wasn't a bad summer to begin with, although it had ended badly for her. For a moment, she became lost in the memories of hanging around in their little gang. Driving around the countryside or just taking trips to the beach. A loud squealing noise brought her out of her reverie; she looked automatically out the window.

A passenger coach slid along the wet tarmac toward the petrol pumps. The driver frantically trying to regain control. Annabel began racing over to the window.

'Marcus, look!' She pointed outside.

They were feet away from it but encased in a cocoon of concrete and glass. What they didn't know was how safe the structure was. Would it manage to stop the out of control coach? Had to, didn't it? Panic filled her as she watched helplessly as the accident unfolded before their eyes.

'Oh God,' was all Marcus said to her. It was like a slow motion movie. A large articulated lorry pulled blindly out in front of the coach.

Screams resonated around the building; the noise of the screeching tires became unbearable. Annabel covered her ears with her hands. There was nothing they could do but stand and watch and wait. The lorry swung around much too quickly, hitting the coach sideways on, carrying it forward toward the building. When the tail end of the lorry caught the fuel pumps, petrol flew up into the air like a fountain, washing the floor, cars, and petrol station on the way back down to earth. The putrid stench of petrol hung heavily in the air.

'We need to do something, Marcus!' Annabel screamed.

'Do what? I may be strong, but even I can't stop a moving coach or a HGV!'

Annabel stayed by the window watching, waiting for what came next. The screams grew louder. They sounded so far away like she was in a tunnel, yet her eyes told a different story. The coach was nearly on top of them, squealing brakes as the two vehicles inched toward them.

'Annabel, move!' She heard someone in the distance scream her name. But Annabel found that her feet were rooted to the spot, she couldn't leave, couldn't take her eyes off the coach.

4

'Move now!' Marcus grabbed Annabel by the hand, dragging her to the far end of the café. 'Annabel!' Marcus shouted as he threw them both on the floor, his body protectively over hers.

A thunderous crack broke through the screams as shards of broken glass flew through the air like bullets out of a gun, landing anywhere they could. The coach inched further into the café, its brakes no longer doing what they should. The coach crashed into the stone pillar in the middle of the café. Finally, both the coach and the lorry ground to a halt.

'Marcus, you saved us.' Her voice came out shaky and unsure.

Marcus looked at where they had been standing. He had moved them just in time.

'It's okay, sweets. You're okay.' He

held her tightly to him. He could feel her heart beating against his chest. Large pieces of concrete fell from the ceiling above them. Lights flickered on and off before crashing to the ground, sending sparks flying in every direction. A sandstorm of dust clouded their vision; Marcus was knocked to the ground by a piece of falling masonry. The screams grew louder and louder. People desperately called for help. The noise was deafening, but silence would have been worse.

★　★　★

'Annabel,' Marcus called to her from somewhere in the darkness.

Annabel picked herself up off the floor, her visibility impaired by the thick blanket of dust. A warm liquid snaked down her face. Wiping it away, she brought her hand toward her, trying to see what it was. All she could see was that it was dark, likely blood. Hopefully not a large cut. 'Marcus.

Where are you?'

She heard a groan. 'Here, I'm okay.' Marcus's voice broke through the blackness like a reassuring light.

Kneeling on the floor, she tried to feel for him. 'Keep talking so I can find you.'

'Annabel, don't worry about me, the people on the coach!'

'I'll need you to help.' Annabel reached out and finally found him. 'Can you stand?'

'Course I can stand. Honestly, woman. I'm not hurt. I only fell over.' Marcus tried to lighten the mood. But now wasn't the time for his daft jokes. He grabbed Annabel's hand as they both stood together holding the other for support. Her whole body shook with fear. Reaching behind her, she felt her backpack. *A good job I didn't take this off. I would never have been able to find it again.*

'Come on. We've got to help.' Her voice stern, the sort that made all the nurses on the ward do exactly as she said. 'Marcus, go and find the waitress. I'll go to the coach.'

★　★　★

Marcus liked how assertive Annabel was being. She was definitely a different person to the one he had known. 'Be careful, my Anna.'

Where the hell had that just come from? She wasn't his Anna anything. *Marcus, keep your mind on the task.* He was hindered by all the debris that was once a café. Tables and chairs were strewn around, and live wires hung down from the ceiling sparking intermittently.

Marcus shouted out, 'Waitress, where are you?' A muffled voice seemed to come from behind the upturned counter. *That sounded bad, but he didn't even know her name.*

He moved chairs and tables out of the way as he climbed through the devastation. Ignoring the searing pain shooting through his body, Marcus peered behind the counter, the waitress who had served them earlier was huddled in the recess. She didn't look hurt, but her whole body was shaking. 'Take my hand. You're all right.'

Marcus inched forward, but his movements caused more concrete to fall from the twisted remains of the café roof. 'Come on, we need to get you outside.'

'My café?' the waitress said.

Okay, so that was the last thing Marcus thought she'd say, but the poor woman was in shock. He had no idea if they would be any safer outside than in. The river of petrol by the pumps could go up any minute, especially if someone was stupid enough to light a match. He had signed up for a charity bike ride, and now here he was playing a hero.

'There's nothing we can do. We have to go.' Marcus grabbed the woman and pulled her to her feet. The sheer effort was too much, and he fell to his knees doubling up in pain. Quickly, he rose to his feet. He had to stop thinking about himself and help the others. Marcus had a vague idea where the front of the café used to be, but the dust and debris and two mangled vehicles made visibility virtually impossible.

'My café.' The poor woman kept repeating herself, and even as he held her hand, he could feel her shaking with fear.

'Annabel?' Marcus shouted. There was no answer; most of the screaming had stopped. 'Annabel?'

'Is that the girl you were with?' the waitress asked.

'Yes, she's a doctor.' Marcus squeezed the waitress's hand for no real reason other than reassurance. Twice he had called out to her, and twice there was only the sickening silence. *She has to be okay.* Where was she? Marcus was suddenly filled with dread; it was too quiet. Was she hurt? Had a piece of concrete fallen on her too? *No, Marcus, you have to think clearly. She is all right. Anna is somewhere in this mess.* It was becoming too hard to think through the thick fog of pain descending over him.

'Mister, are you all right?'

'I'm fine,' Marcus snapped. No, he wouldn't be fine until he had seen Anna. 'We need to call 999.' Marcus couldn't believe that a quick brew at a service station had turned into a rescue mission. It was like something out of a disaster movie from Hollywood. The situations were usually great entertainment, but this was real. People were hurt.

Marcus and the waitress stepped over the twisted metal of the window frame and out into the fresh air. 'What's your name, miss?'

'Kristy. You are?'

'Marcus.'

'Thank you, Marcus.'

Her thanks seemed heartfelt, but before he could say anything else they were surrounded by a mass of people. 'Has anyone contacted the emergency services?' He looked around at the blank faces. What the hell had they all been doing, standing like statues waiting for someone else to do it for them? He had no idea who was saying what. Everyone talked over each other.

Then the chatter started, and that was enough to get him mad.

'Enough,' Marcus shouted, holding his hand up. 'There's people trapped in the coach and the building.'

Everyone stood around not moving but talking about what had just happened. Maybe some were in shock. They had blank expressions on their faces.

Several men suddenly shouted, 'On it, boss,' as they wandered into the devastated building that he had just come from.

So that is what it took, someone to take charge, just like Annabel had with him. There were so many people walking around with cuts to their faces. He didn't know what to do with them, but at least a few cuts were manageable, and they could tell their children and grandchildren how they got them. The ones walking were the least of his worries. The driver was still in the truck and needed help.

He watched as the three men he had sent to help Annabel wandered off in her direction. Marcus went to the truck. The cab end was buried inside the building whilst the cargo it had carried was strewn all over the car park. He didn't notice at first, but then to his horror, he realized they were gas canisters. His eyes darted toward the petrol station. Shiny liquid crept silently along the tarmac.

They had no equipment and no real medical supplies, only what Anna had packed. He recoiled at the memory of him telling her she wouldn't need it. *I hope whatever you have in there will be enough.* Pulling out his mobile, he dialed the emergency services. 'Which service do you require?' asked a posh voice on the other end of the call.

'What do you mean, which service?' Marcus paused a minute to try and compose himself. 'There're people injured, the place could go up in a ball of flames at any moment, and you ask a stupid question.'

'Could you please tell me what has happened?'

'A HGV truck has collided with a passenger coach. The coach is now in the middle of a café, and there is petrol spilling from the petrol station.'

'Okay, help is on its way.'

After he gave directions to the service station, the phone died.

Marcus went back inside the collapsed building. Inching his way to the cab, he hoped the driver would be okay. What if he wasn't? Marcus didn't know what to do. *You can't save anyone, Marcus. You didn't help Emily.* A voice in his head mocked his inability to help his own daughter, stopping him in his tracks. He had to put any melancholy thoughts to one side and help however he could. Once he had done this, he needed to move those gas canisters before they ignited. The whole place would go up then. He banged on the cab window. 'You all right?'

A groan was all the reply he got. Pulling on the door handle wasn't getting him anywhere. He looked around him. He needed something anything to pry the door open. He couldn't risk doing it from the passenger side, live cables hung down on that side. Marcus grabbed the nearest piece of metal and began jimmying the door. It was hard work as beads of sweat appeared on his forehead.

The door suddenly gave way, sending Marcus to the ground. After picking himself up, he yanked the door open. 'Sir, are you all right?'

The truck driver just looked at him blankly. 'What happened?'

'You've been in an accident. We need to move you outside,' Marcus replied kindly.

Marcus checked the man the best he could. He didn't look like there was anything wrong with him, except the cut on his head. Though the driver was in shock, Marcus felt it was safe to move him. Better than staying in an unsafe building about to explode from gas. 'Come on,' he stated as he undid the man's seat belt.

★   ★   ★

Annabel had no idea where Marcus had gone as she tried to smash the coach's door, single-handed. Marcus was never there when she needed him. Men, honestly. She could see the driver slumped over the steering wheel and people writhing around on seats. It didn't look good. She had to get in and help.

'Miss, do you need our help?'

Annabel was grateful to see the three men. 'I need that door off now.'

'Stand back, miss.'

She watched as the men grabbed the nearest piece of concrete and pounded on the glass. Annabel tried to tell the passengers to get down, but half of them looked too terrified to move.

Finally, after a few minutes, they had broken their way through. Annabel gingerly climbed through the hole. A sharp pain pierced her arm as a shard of glass impaled her coat, holding her fast.

A trickle of her own blood ran down her arm. 'Wonderful, just what I need.' Shrugging off the pain, she entered the coach. A lot of the people presented with just cuts and bruises. The passengers at the back gave her more concern. They were too quiet, and the driver of the coach lay slumped over the steering wheel.

Annabel turned to the men that had helped her. 'Look, can you help the passengers with just cuts and bruises get off the coach? I will try and see what the others need.'

'Sure thing,' came the reply.

Annabel walked straight to the rear of the coach. The two passengers at the back had been crushed against the seat in front of them. Neither moved when she talked to them. Taking off her backpack, she then took out her stethoscope and checked to see if they were still breathing. Adrenaline had kicked in as she worked on them both, giving morphine, and placing oxygen masks over their faces, tucking the small oxygen bottles on their knees. She couldn't do much more than wrap their wounds up and try and to stop the bleeding she could see. It was more likely that they had internal damage to their bodies.

'Can one of you see if the fire brigade are here? These two need to be cut out.'

Relief flooded Annabel as all but the three passengers walked unsteadily off the coach and toward the shattered remains of the window. Turning her attention to the driver, she heard a familiar voice behind her.

'Anna!'

'Marcus, you've got to help me try and get the driver off. He's unconscious and, apart from a cut on his head, doesn't seem injured.'

Marcus complied and helped Anna

lift the driver off the bus, laying him down on a cleared bit of surface. There would be nothing to do but sit and wait for the paramedics and fire brigade to come and sort these people out.

'Anna, you look so tired.'

'I am. Early start this morning and now this. Some charity ride I set going.'

'It was a great idea,' Marcus replied. 'Look, perhaps you can tell me more about what's been going on over at the hospital?'

'Yes, when we've sorted this lot out. I've no idea if there is anyone else in the building.'

'I will go check; you stay here,' Marcus ordered.

Annabel thought back to the Marcus she had met that summer. He would help anybody out, but his main passion were his bikes and they came first. She remembered he had once said if he had a choice, a woman or a bike, he would choose a bike every time. She had always wondered why that was.

The loud noise of sirens interrupted

her thoughts. The cavalry was here. Annabel was relieved. She had one bandage and a tube left out of all the supplies she had brought. She could help them if they needed her to, but hopefully, there would be enough paramedics to sort everyone out.

Marcus came back to her a few moments later. 'I can't find anyone, but the amount of concrete that's fallen in here makes it hard to see. There are loads of people outside. Maybe there was another way out.'

'I guess, I just don't want anybody left behind.'

Marcus held her hand. 'There won't be. The emergency service will make sure of that.'

★   ★   ★

Marcus couldn't believe how different Annabel was from the girl he once knew. Even though it was brief, she had never been this sure of herself. Now, here she was taking charge of the situation whilst he felt like a bystander. He was no doctor. Crunching numbers and making people money was one thing; saving people's lives every day was another. He knew they couldn't save everyone, but today Annabel ordered people around in the nicest possible way, doing more than he ever could.

Emily would really have liked her for a mum. Marcus blinked hard. Where had that errant thought come from? They had only just called a truce, and now he was thinking she would have been the perfect mother for his late daughter?

'Marcus, I need you to help.'

'Eh, what did you say, Anna?' Marcus shook himself back to the situation in hand.

'I need you to go and tell the paramedics and fire brigade we need them in here.' Annabel checked the driver's pulse. 'The driver's pulse is slowing. He needs help now.'

'On it, boss.' Marcus did as he was

asked, running over the fallen masonry and out into the daylight. He searched for the ambulance. They were a few meters away from the service station entrance.

So many people mingled everywhere, blocking his path. Marcus did what he used to do before he grew up; he shoved and pushed people out of the way. Seeing a couple of paramedics treating someone with cuts and bruises, he grabbed their arm. 'I need you to help the coach driver.' Marcus struggled to get the words out. 'He's seriously injured, in the building. My girlfriend's with him.'

Anna isn't your girlfriend; get a grip on yourself.

The paramedics grabbed a stretcher and followed him. 'There's two people trapped on the coach too.' How could he have forgotten them? Annabel was running on and off the coach to treat all three. She was an amazing woman; Marcus wasn't sure what was happening to him. When the coach had come toward the window and she still stood there, he was terrified. He didn't want anything to happen to her.

Annabel was back on the coach when he came back. 'Marcus, their condition is deteriorating.'

Marcus didn't even need to say anything. He just turned back around and went for more help, returning a few minutes later with extra hands and firemen with cutting equipment.

'Look, you two. You need to get out of here,' one of the firemen told them.

'I'm a doctor. Don't you need my help?' Annabel was trying to insist that she stay.

'Come on, sweets. You're exhausted and mucky,' Marcus quipped.

'Yes, like you look any better.'

★   ★   ★

She had been grateful for his help, but she was still far from forgiving him. Her entire body tingled when she was close to him. She couldn't trust him with her heart — not after what happened. But Marcus had proved just how reliable and trustworthy he was in an emergency.

A secret smile crossed her lips. Would it be possible, could it be possible that there was something more to him that meets the eye? Had she gotten him wrong all this time? Her mind was in turmoil. She was worried about all the passengers and worried about her own heart. Could she be falling for him after so short a time in his company? Annabel had known Marcus before, the playboy with the love-them-and-leave-them attitude.

The man who stood next to her was different; he had grown, become someone she felt she could spend more time with. Have some fun for once.

Marcus clicked his fingers in front of her face. 'Earth to Anna, come in, Anna.'

'Er, sorry, I was thinking,' she apologized.

'You seem miles away. Let's go

outside. Maybe there is someone you can help.'

★   ★   ★

He had reached her. One thing he was learning was Annabel would be there for anyone. A doctor was always on call. It warmed him. She was definitely special. He wished he had seen it properly before and fought for her; instead, he had let her go and walked away.

As they stepped outside, a cold wind blew suddenly. It felt nice, breathing in some fresh air after being sat in that dusty dangerous atmosphere.

'I'll be back, Marcus,' Annabel said, a hand on his arm.

'Don't go back in there. Promise me, Anna!' He filled with fear.

'I won't, I promise.'

Marcus watched as she walked away from him.

'Don't light that cigarette.' Marcus heard the desperate shout — but it was too late, whoever they were shouting at had already done it.

A fireball leapt into the air as the petrol ignited, scattering people everywhere as they ran for cover. The flames licked and engulfed everything that they touched. Mini explosions sounded as cars that stood wheels deep in the river of petrol went up in flames. Huge plumes of black smoke rose high above their heads as the petrol station ignited. Firemen ran with extinguishers. They sprayed marshmallow foam over the whole area trying to put out the fire.

Marcus was scared when he couldn't see Anna. He searched frantically through the thick black smoke and the crowds to find her.

5

Marcus breathed a huge sigh of relief when he looked into one of the ambulances and saw a calm, cool Annabel helping to treat a patient. The fire brigade had the fire almost under control before everything went up and everybody with it. All he could do was stand back as the emergency services did their jobs. He and Annabel had done as much as possible. They, with others around them, had gotten everyone or at least they thought they had.

He watched as the fire crews sprayed sand on the petrol slick to stop it igniting. Marcus thought how lucky it was nobody had lit another match or else they would have all been blown to kingdom come. Looking through the dust, he spotted what looked like a silver arm, near the back of the café.

'Annabel, we didn't miss anyone, did we?' he asked hastily.

'No. At least I don't think so.' He caught the puzzled look on her face. 'Look in the back' — he pointed to the building — 'there's someone under that concrete.'

'Marcus, just tell the firemen. They will go in.'

Marcus had already decided what he was going to do, dashing past the taped line that had been placed to cordon off the building.

'Oi, you can't go in!'

Marcus heard the stem shout behind him, but chose to ignore it; he couldn't leave anyone trapped in there. He stumbled with each step he took, dodging the live wires, which now hung from the ceiling like hungry animals just waiting to pounce on their next victim.

'Marcus, wait,' a breathless female voice called out to him.

'Go back, Anna. Don't come in.' He waved his hand toward the opening.

'It's not safe. You can't come back in here.'

Marcus carried on. He couldn't worry about her now. He had to get to that arm, to the person trapped helplessly beneath the rubble and dust. Would they be okay? Would they be seriously injured? Marcus had no idea what that person was going to be like. All he knew was he had to be the one to get them out. He couldn't save his daughter, but perhaps he could save one more person here. Suddenly, it was there before him, the silver arm sticking out beneath the rubble. Leaning forward, he took hold of the arm and pulled it a little. Marcus breathed a huge sigh of relief. It was only someone's jacket that they had left behind.

He pulled on it harder, falling backward onto the floor. A loud creaking sounded out. Marcus screamed as a piece of ceiling fell onto his ribs, knocking all the air out of his lungs.

'Marcus!'

Anna was there somewhere in the distance. A dust cloud blew through the hole covering him with debris. 'Anna, I need . . . ' But he couldn't get his words out, it was so hard to breathe. He tried to move the concrete block from his chest, but it was no use. Marcus lay there feeling helpless and alone. Was this where he had been destined to die? He thought he could hear a young girl's tinkling laughter. 'I'm not ready yet, Emily,' he whispered.

★　★　★

'Marcus, where are you?' Annabel shouted out, she had a feeling where he was, but she couldn't see him, couldn't even hear him. Annabel called a few more times and then walked boldly forward, ducking under the wires and climbing over the shattered remains of the café.

'Here,' he called, his voice a faint whisper.

Annabel saw him then, or at least the

71

reflective stripes of his jacket. Her heart raced as she rushed carelessly toward him. The last thing she had ever wanted was for Marcus to be hurt, no matter how badly he had treated her.

Kneeling down, she called to him, 'Marcus, are you okay. Can you stand?'

'I can if you help me push this bit of concrete off,' he replied breathlessly.

Annabel felt along Marcus's body trying to find where the concrete lay. Her pulse quickened as her hands ran up his leg briefly touching his ass. She was scared he would hear the pounding of her heart. Her slow movements were stopped in their tracks by the discovery of a cold hard object. Pushing with all her might, she eventually got the piece of concrete off him. 'Marcus, are you okay?'

'Yes.'

But she noticed his breathing was erratic like he was gasping for breath. Grasping his hand, she helped him back to his feet. Almost immediately, he doubled over in pain.

Annabel thought for a moment and glanced at the jacket he held in his hand. 'I need to take your coat and T-shirt off, Marcus and I see you rescued the jacket.'

'Don't make me laugh. It hurts.' He was becoming more breathless with each second that passed.

'Come on. Let's get your stuff off.'

'Oh yes!' Marcus winked.

'Don't get any ideas. I think you've broken a rib, maybe more. We need to strap it up.' Yanking her backpack off, she then dived in and retrieved a bandage. Wrapping it tightly around Marcus's rib cage, Annabel heard him wince each time the bandage went around his body.

'Good job you brought that along,' he conceded. 'I didn't think it was worth you carrying it all this way.'

Annabel looked at him angrily. 'Well, it's a good job someone thinks of these things.' She noticed that his breathing was still very labored, and each step seemed to be extremely difficult for him. They made slow progress trying to dodge the bits of falling concrete and the large pieces that lay all over the floor. 'All this to rescue a coat.'

'All right, enough of that, thank you.'

'Listen, Mr. Narky, I did tell you. Should have listened to me.' Annabel sounded like a schoolteacher telling off a naughty pupil. 'Come on,' she replied, taking hold of his arm as they slowly and steadily walked outside.

★ ★ ★

'Yes, yes.' Marcus had had enough of Annabel's little digs. That was one thing he had missed about her. She would always tell him how it was, and four years later, Annabel was still the same.

The last thing he was going to do was admit she had been right. It hadn't been a good idea to go back in, not when there were people around wearing the proper safety equipment.

Annabel had let go of his arm. 'You,

go stand over there and out of trouble, whilst I go fetch someone to have a proper look at you.'

'But . . . ' It was too late. Annabel had wandered off in the direction of the ambulances.

Marcus walked slowly over to a group of cars; a snail would have got there faster. His head began to spin. He needed to sit down. He banged into a car allowing his body to slide against the cold paintwork down to the ground. He couldn't breathe. He tried desperately to remove the bandages from around his body. The pain intensified as he did so. He found himself being dragged down into the blackness even though he was trying desperately to fight off the feeling. The hairs on Marcus's neck stood on end. It was getting so cold.

As Marcus lay on the floor, the ground still spun beneath him. Wave after wave of nausea washed over him. Finally, he gave in to the blackness as it consumed him.

Annabel looked around for Marcus, but she couldn't see him. 'Marcus!' She shouted his name but received no reply. Incessant chatter from everyone else made it difficult to hear anything.

She thought of the last place she had seen him. He had been walking toward some cars. Marcus hadn't looked great. Maybe he had just gone to find a place to sit down. She raced over to the furthest part of the car park and checked around the dozens of cars. They were still blocked in and had nowhere to go to. They couldn't leave until the police said it was okay.

Annabel checked all around the cars, nothing. *Where are you, Marcus?* She ran back toward the ambulances to see if he was anywhere near them. Could he be chatting to some of the people injured? Trying to keep them calm, she stopped a paramedic. 'Have you seen a guy in black leathers come past?'

'No, sorry, love, we haven't. Got our

hands full, we have,' he replied stiffly.

She stood still for a moment turning around in a circle. Where the hell was he? 'Marcus!' She shouted as loud as she could, but over this din with sirens blaring out and loads of people stood around chatting, her voice didn't carry. There was one more group of cars left to try. After that, Annabel had no idea what to do. He hadn't given her his phone number, so she couldn't ring him and find him that way.

Her whole body was cold with fear. What if he really was hurt and not just with a few broken ribs? She hadn't had a chance to examine him properly. It had been too hectic to get everyone out of the coach and to safety. Annabel knew she herself needed stitches as blood continued to seep through her clothes. She hadn't checked the cars near the fallen building.

Please, please, be all right, Marcus. I couldn't cope if anything happened to you. Would he hear her silent prayer? Annabel dashed to the cars. She couldn't see him, but then she stopped dead. Marcus lay on the ground, his eyes closed, his chest barely moving. *Oh God, no.* Her hands flew over her mouth. 'No, Marcus,' she screamed at him.

Kneeling down by his side, she listened to his breathing. It was labored and shallow. Annabel had a sinking feeling his broken ribs had punctured his lung as well. Leaning over, she unzipped his jacket and tried removing it as best she could away from his waist. Annabel's hands shook as she pulled his T-shirt up over his taut stomach. 'Please don't leave me,' she whispered into his ear.

Annabel hoped that wherever Marcus was, he could hear her. After taking her backpack off, she searched frantically for her scalpel and a piece of tubing. She would have to cut his side, underneath his arm and try to inflate his lung back up, draining any fluid. She had no anesthetic with her, just some morphine. 'Please forgive me.'

She gave him a shot of morphine. Using her fingers, she guided the scalpel and cut an incision into his side, threading the tube slowly and steadily into his lung. 'Get the paramedics,' she shouted to one of the many people standing around helplessly watching.

Annabel had no idea how the paramedics managed to lift Marcus onto the stretcher, but they managed it. She couldn't leave his bike here; she didn't even know where here was.

There was a loud rumbling noise as a stream of bikers poured into the destroyed services, pulling to a stop near Annabel.

'Dr. Simpson, where's Marcus?'

'He's got to go to hospital with a punctured lung and fractured ribs.' She dug in his pockets for his bike key.

'Look, please take this and get his bike back to Brighton.'

'No problem. Everything will be cool.'

Annabel had no idea who the biker was, just that he was friends with her

Marcus. *No, come on. He isn't your Marcus.*

'Miss, we really need to get your boyfriend to the hospital.'

'I'm not his girlfriend, and it's Dr. Simpson. Take him back to Brighton.'

'I'm sorry, Doctor, isn't Southampton nearer?' the paramedic apologized. Any more nodding and he would be bowing.

'You will only have to transport him back in a few days. Take him to Brighton,' Annabel replied, her voice stern and cold.

'Yes, Doctor,' the paramedics said in unison.

Annabel didn't think they were too happy about it, but she didn't care. She wanted to personally oversee Marcus's care, and she couldn't very well do it away from where she lived or worked. This way, he was in easy reach.

Climbing into the ambulance was a huge relief. After all the devastation and panic, now there was a calm efficiency that only the paramedics seemed able to give. Annabel was still concerned for Marcus, but he would fare much better in the hands of a surgeon.

★   ★   ★

Marcus tried to open his eyes and emerge from the darkness, but it was not ready to release him from its grip. He could hear voices in the distance, just a quiet rumbling. He couldn't make out what they were saying. A small chink of light intruded on the darkness. Marcus's head pounded. He willed himself to sit up, but his body remained unresponsive to the demands that his brain was sending. He tried to move his arms, but they were like lead, and no matter how hard Marcus tried, he couldn't move them on demand.

Marcus heard the door close. Bright light intruded into his darkness, but instead of disappearing as it had before, it stayed. His head and his entire body ached even more. Someone needed to turn off that damn light. Whoever had decided to leave it on had to be out to punish him.

The male and female voices he heard didn't sound like they wanted to hurt him. Marcus tried to move his fingers. At first, they were stiff, but after several minutes, he could bend them. Willing his eyelids to open, he saw the bright light that intruded on his darkness. The effort exhausted him. Marcus drifted in and out of sleep — at least he thought he was sleeping. He hadn't heard the strange voice for a while. Where had it gone? Was he alive or was this heaven?

Determination swept over him. He didn't like this dark place, and he was desperate to see the sky, the sun. As his eyelids slowly opened, the light became brighter until it was a constant presence. Turning his head, he could see shapes; they were blurry at first, but as he concentrated, everything came into focus. He smiled triumphantly. Turning his head to one side, he saw Annabel sleeping in a chair next to his bed, her hand in his.

'Anna,' he whispered. Marcus didn't want to wake her. She looked so peaceful, her head bent slightly to one side. His whole body ached for a moment. He wondered why, then a sharp pain in his side alerted him to the reason.

Annabel moaned in response as her eyes fluttered open. 'Marcus, you're awake.'

'Yes, but I hurt like hell.'

'You will. I had to cut you yesterday and insert a tube. You'll be staying in hospital for a few days before being allowed home.' Annabel pulled her hand out of Marcus's, her face filled with embarrassment.

'Oh, I see. Because you never got to finish your brew, you decide to operate on me.' Marcus tried to laugh, but he cried out in pain.

'Marcus, try not to make any sudden movements.'

'Have you been here all night, sweets?' he said, his voice so low it was almost a growl.

'Yes, someone had to keep an eye on you.'

'Thanks, for being here.' He didn't know which way to take it. At least they weren't shouting. 'Where am I anyway?'

'You're back in Brighton. I thought it would be easier and no need to transport you back when you were feeling better.'

Marcus nodded his agreement; he didn't seem too bothered either way. He was glad it hadn't been anything serious. Or had it? Oh well. Whatever had happened, at least Anna was there with him. He hadn't done or said too much wrong to make her walk away.

Just then, the door opened and an oldish gentlemen walked in with a stethoscope around his neck. 'I'm glad to see you awake, Mr. Chapman.' The doctor picked up the chart at the end of the bed. 'I hope you realize just how lucky you were yesterday.'

'Er, no.' *Bang goes that theory.* 'To be honest, I can just remember the crash and helping people. After that, it's all a bit of a blur,' Marcus admitted.

'Well, you've had a pneumothorax.' The doctor looked at him straight in the eyes.

Marcus stared back, utterly confused. Whatever the doctor just said sounded bad. It was very uncomfortable, whatever he had done. His ribs were strapped up so tightly, he was having trouble breathing.

'In layman's terms, you broke several ribs, and one of your ribs punctured your lung.' The doctor placed the chart back at the end of the bed. 'We've inflated it and want to keep you in hospital for a couple of days, and then you can go home. No strenuous exercise, rest and relaxation, healthy food.'

'That explains why I feel like I have been hit by a wrecking ball,' Marcus quipped. 'Great, no riding for a while. I was just beginning to enjoy that again.' Marcus frowned, but there was one perk to being sick — Anna was at his side. Just like it always should have been.

'I am sorry, Mr. Chapman, but bikes are totally out of the question for the time being.'

'Yes, Doctor.' *Yes, now I have rediscovered the joys of my motorbike, I am definitely not going to give it up.*

'Well, I will leave you two to it,' the doctor replied and left quietly.

Annabel waited until he had gone. 'You know he's right. You need to completely relax for a while.'

'Anna, can we talk please?' he implored her.

'What about?'

'The past?' Marcus added quietly.

'There's no point in revisiting that.' Annabel stood and walked slowly to the door. 'I've got to get back to work.'

'No, you don't. You took the weekend off, and it's Saturday. You're not back at work till Monday.' Marcus moved a little too much, wincing in pain.

'Why do you want to bring it all up? I was embarrassed enough back then. It

86

will only make it worse.'

Marcus stared intently into her face. 'Just tell me why you never called.' He saw Annabel's face contort.

'How the hell was I meant to phone? I didn't have your number.' Her voice rose slightly.

He shook his head. 'Yes, you did. I scrawled it down on that takeaway box we'd had.'

'A takeaway box! You wrote your number on something I was going to throw away?' For a moment, Annabel was speechless. 'Have you never heard of paper or even staying till I had woken up?'

Annabel's dig hit its mark as Marcus flinched at how she must have felt he had abandoned her. They had spent a wonderful night making love, and when the call about his grandma had come, he had to leave. He had no choice. What had he done to the one girl who had given him everything and he had given her nothing in return? 'You try finding a piece of paper in that dump of a flat. There was stuff everywhere.'

'Oh great, so not only did you leave me high and dry, but you're having a dig about my flat too.' Annabel got up to leave.

He tried to hold his arms out to stop her leaving. 'Look, don't go. Sit back down, and let's discuss this, and at least pretend we're adults.'

Shaking him off, Annabel sat back down. 'I guess it was messy back then,' she conceded. She certainly wasn't going to tell him her house was pretty much as the flat had been.

'My gran was rushed into hospital. That's why I left.'

Annabel listened. Was he telling the truth? His voice didn't waver, and he was looking straight at her with those gorgeous blue-gray eyes of his. Someone had once told her that the eyes never lie, just look into them, and she would see.

He placed his hand on hers, sending a shiver down her spine. 'I came back a few days later, but you had gone. No one would tell me what uni you were at.'

Somehow, Annabel thought he hadn't looked very hard either. 'What happened then happened. I was a convenient notch on your bedpost. A deranged woman you saw as an easy lay.'

Marcus raised his voice several octaves. 'You are not now nor were you ever a notch on my bedpost!' Disgust etched his face.

She had always assumed that is what she had been.

'I can't believe your opinion of me is so low.'

'I . . . I — '

'Your comment shows me just what you really thought of me.' Marcus stared out of the window. He wanted to know how she had formed such a bad opinion of him.

'Marcus, I'm sorry I assumed — '

'I know what you assumed.' Had Annabel been so naïve? 'You were so unlike any of the others.' He wasn't going to tell her that she was the one he wanted to be with. That she had left him alone just as he had been falling in love with her. Then Josie had come along and caught him at his lowest ebb. Annabel had disappeared, and Josie was his rebound girl. But Emily, his little girl, now, she was the best thing to ever happen to him. Should he tell Annabel? Would she even understand why he had done what he had?

She looked utterly embarrassed. Had she really made him into the bad guy without even checking her facts?

'I'm so sorry, I . . . '

'Look, come here,' Marcus said, patting the bed.

Annabel approached cautiously. Had it really been a misunderstanding? They had wasted so much time; maybe, just maybe, they had a chance to sort this out.

'Marcus.' She touched his face with her hand, and electricity arched between them.

Was she too shy to ask for what she

wanted, too scared to make the first move?

Marcus lifted his arm up and snaked his hand around her neck, ignoring the pain that he felt. He moved Annabel's face to his until he could feel her hot breath on his face. Brushing her lips gently with his, and when she didn't pull away, he deepened the kiss. Marcus needed her. He had to show her just what she had always meant. Twisting his fingers into her hair, he held her tight against him.

When she wrapped her arms around his neck, Marcus sensed she was being careful not to hurt him. He was dizzy, and his whole body tingled with anticipation. The noises he had heard a few minutes before from the corridor vanished. In that one moment, it was just the two of them, in their own world.

A white heat filled his belly as he tried to keep hold of his sanity and not get carried away with a knee-weakening kiss. Marcus didn't know how much more he could take.

What he wanted more than anything was to run his hands all over her for their hearts to beat as one, as their lips danced to an unheard tune.

6

Marcus pulled away, wincing in pain.

'I'm sorry, I'm sorry,' Annabel gasped pulling back quickly, horrified she might have hurt him.

'Shh, I'll survive.' Subdued pain laced his quiet chuckle. 'I got a little . . . carried away too.' Marcus couldn't believe his luck! Annabel had kissed him back with as much passion as he felt for her. 'When I get out of here, do you want to do something?'

Annabel smiled. 'Yes, I'd love to,' she said while sitting back in the chair at the side of the bed, 'as long as it's a quiet something. We've had enough excitement for a while.'

'I wonder how they're all getting on with the ride.'

'I'm not sure. I will give them a ring and tell you later.' Annabel glanced at her watch and let out a heavy breath. 'I need to run.' The dull throbbing from her wound had become a toothed monster in the last couple of hours. She could no longer ignore her own need for sutures and clean bandages.

'My bike?' Marcus's loud shout shocked her.

'Don't worry. Someone is bringing it back to Brighton.' Annabel stared at the wall for a moment. 'Not sure what condition it will be in after the ride.'

'Oh, okay. It's just that it's a classic, and I wouldn't want anything to happen to it.'

Annabel laughed harshly. 'You've suffered a serious injury, and all you're concerned about is getting your bike back in one piece.' His priorities seemed a bit out of whack.

'Well, I love my bike more than any woman,' he retorted.

'Not surprising.'

'Look, no one comes between a man and his toys.'

'That death trap isn't a toy.'

Annabel was conflicted. She still didn't like motorbikes but had to admit the feeling of freedom was liberating. 'Marcus, what exactly do you do for a living? I mean, to be able to afford a bike like that?'

'It's boring really,' said Marcus, looking down at his hands. 'I make people money. And lots of it. I started out as an accountant and went from there.'

'Do you still do that?' Annabel paused as Marcus looked up at her. 'Accounts, I mean?'

'Yes, I do my own and for a couple of friends. Why?'

'Oh, it's probably nothing. I might need your help later.'

'You only have to ask,' came his reply.

Annabel was relieved she had someone to help, but in reality she so wanted to be wrong. The horrible niggling feeling kept eating away at her. She looked at Marcus. He looked so tired that overstaying her welcome wasn't a good idea.

'You need to rest, Marcus.' Annabel moved against the bed, taking his hand in hers. 'I will come back later to check on you.'

'No, don't leave yet. Tell me what is worrying you.'

'Well, do you know the hospital is shutting the children's ward?' Annabel asked.

'Yes.'

'There's something strange going on. I can't explain. I don't know.' Annabel ran her hand through her hair in frustration. 'Not yet. I might learn something later.'

'You know I will do anything to help you.'

'Tell me about you. What has my bad boy biker been doing for all these years?' Annabel cringed. She'd let his old nickname slip.

'Nothing much. After that summer, I knew it was time to get serious. I was nearly thirty, and I was still out having fun. It's lucky I owned my own business. Otherwise, I would have got the sack for taking the whole summer off.'

She loved the little naughty school-boy smirk he had just given her. 'Why did you never marry?'

Marcus suddenly looked uncomfortable. 'I just never found the right person.'

Leaning over, she kissed him tenderly before she left the room.

Annabel pressed her back against the wall just outside Marcus's room. What just happened? She had just become comfortable with the idea of reestablishing a friendship with the man. That foundation was still unstable. *Do I want a relationship? Do I want to chance ruining* — no, no, no, she chided herself. Marcus wasn't marrying or boyfriend potential. She dipped her chin to her chest and shook her head. Her fist balled at her sides, and her teeth grated together. She couldn't think straight anymore. She perked up, righting her posture, and giving herself a firm nod. *Paperwork. I have loads of paperwork, which means loads of time to think through this mess!*

She really had to get her arm seen to before she did anything else. Perhaps the nurses on this floor could do it. The only problem she could see would be if she did have glass embedded in the wound. Annabel spotted one of the nurses.

'Do you have a minute, nurse?' she enquired.

'Certainly, Doctor.' The young nurse seemed pleasant enough, her uniform a lighter blue than everyone else's. *A trainee, well she will do.*

'I cut my arm. Is there a chance you could clean it up for me, please?' Annabel used her sternest ward voice.

'Certainly, just come with me.'

They entered a small hospital room, fully equipped with everything the nurse would need. Annabel winced as she took her coat and t-shirt off. Blood had congealed, sticking her top to her body. *Wonderful. My favorite t-shirt ruined.*

The nurse set to work cleaning the wound with sterile water, and after making sure there wasn't any glass, stitched it up. Annabel was relieved that she had received a painkilling injection to numb the area. Now she could get back on with her job. Half a day spent not working was enough to drive her insane, at least she had an excuse, and now she could happily go back to work without feeling like her arm was trapped in a vise.

Her footsteps echoed off the walls as Annabel wandered down to the lifts, to reach her floor. Mr. Wild appeared out of nowhere. It was very uncharacteristic of him to be near the ICU. He didn't normally come into the wards unless to check on supplies. *Just as slippery as a snake, aren't you, Mr. Wild?*

'Am I to assume by your presence in the hospital, your charity bike ride hasn't happened then?' he sneered.

'It has, actually,' Annabel retorted.

'So why are you back so early?' Mr. Wild looked at her in disgust. 'You aren't going to win against me, Dr. Simpson. Found yourself a new job yet?' He turned away for a moment and then looked back at her. 'Don't forget that I will need to bank all your charity money.'

'No, you're not touching that money.' She jammed her hand in her jeans pocket. 'I am not going to find another job either. You will be the one leaving and looking for a new job.'

'I would love to see you try and stop me with either.' Mr. Wild stepped into the lift. He turned to face the open doors. 'We shall see who wins, Dr. Simpson,' he warned just as the doors closed.

Annabel waited for the next lift. 'What are you up to, Wild?' Why was he so certain he was going to get rid of her? Marcus might be able to help, but how could he help when she didn't even know what Mr. Wild was up to? How much did she want Marcus to be involved with something that was clearly hospital politics?

Whatever happened, there was one thing Annabel knew for sure — Mr. Wild was not getting his hands on the money they had raised to keep the children's ward open. *Who did Mr. Wild think he was saying would be the one to put it in the bank?*

She would ask Margaret Higginbottom for some time in her busy schedule this afternoon. The stern and old-fashioned woman was one of the many board members. While she wasn't someone you wanted to invite over for Sunday dinner, she'd done several interviews with the papers, trying to help Annabel keep the children's ward open. The rest of the board sat on the fence about the whole issue. If they couldn't figure out why there wasn't any money, Annabel wouldn't be able to, at least not on her own.

Once a meeting had been arranged, she tried phoning Rachel to see how the ride was going and to tell her what had happened between her and Marcus. The call went straight to voicemail, so

Annabel left her friend a message. Hopefully, at the next rest stop, Rachel would phone her back, if she wasn't too busy with her hunky biker friend.

Now all she had to do was kill time until four o'clock when Margaret showed up in her office. Annabel took a look around her office. There was paperwork strewn over her desk and medical journals in every corner. It seemed like a good time for a bit of a cleanup. The time she spent with her patients took away from maintaining her office, but with a bit of time on her hands and some excess energy to burn, maybe it was time to make her office reflect her approach to healthcare. The firm knock on her door came as she put away her last journal.

'Come in,' Annabel shouted.

'Dr. Simpson. How very nice to see you,' Margaret replied.

'Thanks for coming on such short notice. I need to ask you something that's puzzling me.' Annabel let out a breath she didn't know she'd been holding. 'I'm wondering where all the money has gone for the children's ward.'

'I'm not sure. We have a third-party company buying the equipment. But otherwise, there shouldn't be any problems.'

Margaret had garnered Annabel's attention. 'A separate company buying medical equipment? That is strange.'

'No, not at all. It is done so we do not get money for equipment mixed up with the money for the running costs.'

Margaret's condescending tone always raised Annabel's hackles. As usual, Annabel was thankful when their conversation concluded. She watched Margaret leave her office as quickly as she came in.

Annabel sank into her chair, leaning her head back to stare at the ceiling tiles. Something was hurting Marcus. Something he wouldn't share with her. What happened to his bravado and selfish attitude? He rarely laughed, and when he did, the laugh didn't reflect in his eyes. *What are you hiding, Marcus?*

It pained her to admit it, but she needed him. The trust issue — could she trust him? She was running out of people and places to turn.

Goose bumps had broken out on her arms when she'd thought of him, and they showed no signs of going away. Annabel sighed; she had had enough of work for the day. The staff knew where to find her. Perhaps a shower and a change of clothes would make her feel better. Then she'd come back, see how Marcus was getting on, and make sure he ate his dinner. She laughed to herself — it was hard to stop playing doctor even when she was off duty.

Gathering her coat from the back of the door, she turned off the lights and headed out the door, still thinking about the day. Annabel had more questions in her mind than answers.

What was Marcus hiding? Where was the money for the children's ward? How much did Margaret know? And could she trust Marcus enough to tell him her suspicions? What with all the hassle she was having with Mr. Wild and Marcus in hospital, Annabel was finding it hard to know which way to turn.

Rachel was doing lates tonight, so there was no way she could talk to her about anything. Marcus had been on her mind ever since she had left him. He was a playboy and a very sexy one at that, but just how far could she trust him? Sometimes, when you see and hear bad things all the time, you start to believe it.

She had never thought that he would notice her that summer. Her friend's brother used to hang around with Marcus's gang, and they tagged along. She had been accepted readily into the group, but as soon as she saw those eyes, that crooked I'm-ready-to-be-bad smile, the I'm-going-to-take-you-to-bed smile, Annabel had fallen head over heels in love with him.

Marcus never encouraged her. She wasn't sure if she had made her feelings obvious to him. Annabel shook her head. 'He would have been a fool not to have seen it,' she said to herself. Instead, Marcus had a stream of girls after him, and he was always happy to take them into his bed but never her. She had to stand by and watch his revolving door of girls that poured in and out of his life. She had lost count of the number he had slept with. Marcus would always say, 'If it's being offered, I'm going to take it.'

Did he know how much hurt he caused her, how many nights she had spent crying over him? As the summer drew to a close, Marcus started paying her attention, but not until the night before she left to complete her final year at university did she spend one blissful night with him.

When she had woken up the next morning, Marcus had gone after getting what he wanted, and she had given it to him on a silver platter. Annabel hadn't bothered getting in touch with him — not that she knew how even if she'd wanted to. Making a clean break had hurt.

Now here she was, all these years later, falling for him all over again, but this time he would never know. She would play him at his own game. A fling, that's what they could have. A no-strings-attached fling. A no-one-would-get-hurt, no-one-would-fall-in-love fling.

Annabel decided not to go home right away but to go see Marcus. Would he be angry with her for kissing him? She needed to see him, just to see. If he told her he never wanted to see her again, then she would have to leave it at that. Perhaps it would be the best thing. Annabel wasn't sure if she wanted to know what he held so close to his chest. Could it be so bad that it would hurt her more?

She knocked lightly on his door before walking in. The nurses had sat him up and positioned his tea tray in front of him. The smell of food was turning her stomach, and it didn't look that appetizing. 'I see you've got your tea.'

Marcus pulled his face at her. 'Is that what you call it?'

Annabel snickered. 'In a fashion.'

'I tell you what, you eat it then,' Marcus replied.

He wasn't too impressed that she had made fun of him. 'Look, Marcus, you need to eat some. If you don't, they won't let you out tomorrow or the day after.'

'Humph.' He stabbed at the food with his fork. 'I bet you say that to everyone.'

'No, it's true. A mean hospital rule, and as you're a patient . . . ' Annabel walked toward the bed and sat down. ' . . . that applies to you as well.'

'I know, you try some, then I will have some.' Marcus was frowning.

'Okay, give me the fork.'

She took it but only put a small bit of food on it. Annabel regretted it almost immediately. It tasted horrible. Who could eat such rubbish? She wanted to kiss him again but shied away as he hadn't made any effort to kiss her again.

'I don't see why I should speak to you anyway,' Marcus said suddenly.

'Why?' Annabel didn't know what she had done. She felt a sinking feeling in the pit of her stomach. Perhaps coming back wasn't such a good idea after all.

'Well, before you left, you gave me a kiss. This time you've walked into my room, tasted my food, and not paid me for it.'

Annabel smiled. 'And what sort of payment does sir require?'

'A kiss should cover it.' He smiled back at her. 'For now, at least.'

Annabel's stomach flipped over. She hesitated for a second. Why would he want to? At least he didn't hate her after all. 'I thought — '

'Just shut up and come here,' Marcus growled.

Leaning over, she kissed him gently, but what she really wanted was to lie in his arms. Her whole body felt like it was on fire. She had no idea how one small kiss could stoke the flames of passion.

Marcus pulled away. 'Push that stupid thing out of the way, and lie next to me.'

'It's not allowed. I can't — I mean . . . '

'Just do it. I want you next to me. The pain can go hang. You're the best cure for me.'

'I . . . I . . . ' Annabel stuttered.

'You still owe me from my meal.' Marcus's eyes sparkled with mirth.

Unsure, Annabel pushed the table away. He wouldn't be able to solve this particular problem for her. Anna was scared he was moving too fast for her. The Marcus of old didn't know what taking things slow meant. He could not be interested in someone like her.

'My Anna,' he groaned as he attempted to turn on his side.

'Wait, I will help.' Annabel rushed to his bed and helped turn him over. He still looked extremely uncomfortable.

'Lie next to me,' he suggested seductively.

Annabel lay next to him, putting her arm over Marcus as carefully as she could.

'You know this is against policy,' she murmured.

'If you can't break the rules once in a while . . . '

Annabel hated to admit that he was right. 'I guess I have conformed to whatever rule had been laid down, done whatever was expected of me.'

'See, there you go. You used to have fun. What's made you so serious?'

Annabel thought for a moment. 'I guess that summer with us and the way it turned out. I mean, don't get me wrong, I have dated since but decided that men were a waste of time.'

'That's nice.' He seemed even unhappier. Annabel couldn't remember turning into the person she was now. It was a rude awakening and one that she didn't want to admit.

'Being in charge of the ward means I

have a lot of responsibilities as well as paperwork. It doesn't leave much time for fun or friends.'

Had Marcus detected the hint of sadness in her voice? He was nice to talk to and beautiful. Marcus closed his eyes with a smile plastered on his face.

It wasn't long before Annabel heard his gentle snoring as he slept. She was as exhausted as he was. It hadn't been very comfortable sleeping in the chair. Annabel let her eyes flutter shut. It was the last thing she remembered until someone shouted at her.

'Excuse me, what on earth are you doing on the patient's bed?' the nurse who had just walked in the room demanded.

Annabel woke with a start. 'I'm sorry, I know.' She untangled herself from Marcus's grip as he continued to sleep through the disturbance. Scrambling off the bed, Annabel thought it was better she went home and had a shower. She would sleep in her own bed and come back tomorrow.

'Look, can you just tell him I will be back tomorrow?'

The nurse just nodded, giving Annabel a stern look. 'You should know better, Doctor.'

With that last dig, Annabel was left alone. It was all very much like a dream. Marcus had playfully told her to kiss him as payment for food. Annabel hadn't known what reception she would get from him. She had expected him to regret they had kissed. Her heartbeat was still erratic as she looked at his sleeping form. Maybe they did have a chance, but one thing was certain, she wouldn't tell him how she was feeling. Kissing Marcus on his temple, she left as quietly as possible. She didn't like the thought of him waking up without her there.

Just as Annabel was walking into the hospital car park, her phone rang.

'Hello?' she answered.

A low voice spoke on the other end. 'Check your emails.'

Annabel heard a click as the line

went dead. She turned quickly to look behind her, and then knelt down to look underneath the cars to see if someone hid away. Was this someone's idea of a joke? She couldn't see anybody nor hear anyone. 'Well done, Rach. You had me going for a second,' Annabel said to herself.

She was curious and would make a point of checking emails when she got home, and the sooner she was out of the car park, the better she would feel. It was as if someone was watching her. Was she in trouble or was there more to this? Things were getting stranger by the minute, and her trust in people was diminishing rapidly.

Marcus was asleep and that was a good thing; perhaps she could take a few more days off and look after him at his hotel. Annabel made a mental note to ask him when she went to see him tomorrow.

It was late by the time she arrived home. Every traffic light she came to seemed to be on red, hindering her progress. She was tired and felt grubby after the past few days. A soak in a nice hot bubble bath would be just the thing to ease her shattered nerves.

Annabel went straight upstairs, knocking a book flying. She had left it on the top step for whatever reason. *Oh well, I will go rescue it later*. She thought back to her flat. Marcus had been right. It had been a mess, or organized chaos as she liked to call it. How would he have found anything in there if he hadn't lived there? It was a hard realization to come to that she had, in fact, been to blame for her own heartbreak.

Heading to her room, she went in and turned on the laptop. She wanted to know if what the man on the phone had said was right. *Check your emails. It will tell you everything*. Her screen flickered to life, a little box at the bottom alerting her to the fact she had mail. Annabel hesitated. Did she really want to open it? The mouse hovered above it for several seconds.

Taking the plunge, she opened the email and was horrified to find a strange message and even stranger log in details.

Dr. Simpson,
The following codes will give you access to all hospital accounts. It would be best to make copies.
A friend

7

The email address didn't look real, as though someone had made a name up just so they could send her this information. *How would anyone get my email?* Then Annabel remembered she had given it to the radio, and it had been read out to a few thousand people live on air.

Loading the printer with paper, she printed the email and then found the hospital site. Following directions, she gained access to all the hospital accounts for the past couple of years. *Who the hell sent me these?* Hitting print, she hoped that whatever was on them would make sense to someone. Marcus hopefully. Maybe a meal would be payment enough. Would he be able to find anything wrong?

It was no use her thinking about things like this. She had to relax and take time to recoup.

Marcus woke a few hours later. The lights in the corridor streamed under the gap in his door, and Annabel was gone. He wanted to phone her see if she was okay but didn't want to push too hard too soon. Annabel would belong to him soon enough. He had no intention of letting her go this time.

There was quite a lot of noise in the corridor, and Marcus assumed that it was nighttime visiting hours. No one else would come to see him, so maybe he should try and get some more sleep.

'Marcus, can I come in?' A middle-aged lady peeped her head around the door.

'Mrs. Windbourne, what a pleasant surprise.' Marcus was genuinely pleased to have a visitor.

'We're not at work now, you know. That nice young doctor who went on that bike ride called me and told me you were here.' She shut the door behind her. 'What on earth have you been doing this time?'

'Not much, just involved in a big accident,' he replied lightheartedly. 'Going to rescue a coat. Getting smashed by falling concrete. You know, all the run-of-the-mill things.' He tried to laugh but instead winced.

'Tut tut, young man. You should be taking better care of yourself. Whatever will I tell your mother?' Mrs. Windbourne shook her head in mock disgust.

'You can't tell her anything, and besides, she's living in Spain.' That was one thing he was grateful for. 'By the time she gets a flight, I will be at home and on the mend.'

'All right, I won't say anything. Now tell me all about this young woman of yours.'

'Annabel is thirty, head of the children's ward, and a really nice down-to-earth person.' Marcus believed everything he had just said. She was special; there weren't many Annabels around who would do anything for others, including putting her own life at risk by coming for him.

'Are you going to see her again?'

'Playing Mum?' Marcus had to smile. It was nice his parents' old neighbor cared enough about him.

'No, I just know what a kind-hearted boy you are.'

'Mary, you will make me blush.'

'Well, if I can't embarrass you, who can?' Mary got up to leave. 'You get some rest, and I will see you in the office in a few days and not before.' Taking a card out of her pocket, she gave it to him.

'Thank you.' Marcus smiled. His wonderful secretary and neighbor had just given him Annabel's phone number. 'Cancel everything for the next week and take some time off yourself. You deserve it for putting up with me.' Marcus would have hugged her if she hadn't been too far away.

'I wouldn't have it any other way, my boy.'

Mary wandered out of the room, and Marcus was left alone to reflect on how a simple ride had turned into a nightmare. His prized bike was who knows where, and in what condition, he had no idea. Okay, so it had been stuck in a garage for a year gathering dust, but now that it was out, he wasn't going to stop riding it. The one thing that bothered him was Annabel; he didn't deserve to be happy. He should have noticed the rash on Emily sooner. Perhaps then she might still be alive.

Marcus pulled the cord. 'I need a phone, please.'

'I will bring you one.'

Marcus sat back and waited. He would give Annabel a ring, just to see if she was okay. She had seemed really distracted when she had left him.

The nurse came back a few minutes later bringing with her a cordless phone. Marcus dialed her number and waited, it rang several times before Annabel answered it.

'Annabel, I just wanted to know if

. . . if you were okay.' He picked at the sheet covering him. 'You just seemed worried earlier.'

'It's nothing, Marcus, honest.'

'What do you mean a strange phone call?' Marcus paused. 'Can you get me out of here tomorrow?'

'No, I'm fine. It's nothing that I can't live with.'

'You don't sound fine. Talk to me, tell me what is wrong.'

'I don't think over the phone is the best place to.'

'Well, get me out of here.'

'Yes, yes, okay, bye.'

When Marcus put the phone down, he was even more worried. What had Anna gotten herself into? By the time he fell asleep, it was almost dawn. The birds twittered away, and movement in the corridor had increased.

★　★　★

Annabel had spent most of the night going over the accounts, but she couldn't see what was wrong. All the money seemed to be accounted for, though looking after money had never been her forte. She barely had enough to pay the bills. Even being in charge of a ward, she was still on a low pay grade when she should have been on a higher one. Mr. Wild had always said they couldn't afford more. Looking at how much the hospital actually had, Annabel knew he had lied, but why? And the question remained, where was the money?

Annabel slung a pair of jeans and a black jumper on and headed straight to the hospital. Marcus had seemed concerned about her, and she would break him out of the hospital. No one would go against a doctor. There was nothing they could do now. His body would have to heal itself, and strong painkillers would help with his pain. Maybe whilst she was at it, she would take a few days off. It may do her some good. All she had done over the past few weeks was rash around. Annabel had no idea who had sent the email. Were they a friend or someone luring her into a trap? The ride was going on until Monday, so she could always stay off till Wednesday. Only if they could cope without her. Annabel didn't want to leave the staff shorthanded.

Annabel arrived at Marcus's room just as the doctor was leaving. 'Doctor Kerry, is the patient safe to leave hospital?'

'Yes, I have advised him that another few days in hospital would be better.' The doctor looked at his watch. 'But you can't tell some people; anyway, I need to get on with the rest of my rounds.'

After knocking quietly on the door, she waited until Marcus told her to come in. It was her right to walk in, but something stopped her. It seemed wrong somehow. Her lips still tingled from the kisses they had shared. Annabel was surprised that her body was so responsive to his. She hadn't wanted to leave him yesterday. *Damn doctors and their bloody rules.* Annabel giggled. *You are one of those doctors with daft rules.*

Annabel opened the door. 'Let's get you out of here,' she said, looking over her shoulder one last time before she closed the door.

'What's wrong, Anna?'

Annabel froze for a moment. 'We will talk in the car; it's not safe here.'

'You're scaring me,' Marcus replied.

'It's nothing. I just don't wanna be overheard.' Annabel took his coat out of the locker. 'You worry too much.'

He walked unsteadily toward her, putting his arms around her waist. 'Do I get a kiss first?'

'You still — '

Marcus didn't allow her to finish what she was going to say. Instead, he crushed his lips against hers. His heart soared as Annabel responded hungrily. He felt her body tremble in his arms. The pain in his ribs increased. It was going to be a long road, but at least Annabel would be at his side.

Reluctantly he pulled away. 'Of course I do.'

The words hung in the air as an unspoken understanding was reached between them. Marcus just wished Annabel would have faith in him, but he had done little to restore it. Hiding Emily's existence would be a cause of some hurt for Annabel because he had lied. Marcus didn't like feeling confused and so unsure of himself. Annabel was his perfect partner, but there was so much between them, so much he was keeping secret.

'Where do you want to go?'

'The Grand,' Marcus answered softly.

'The Grand! How very suave,' she replied teasingly.

'Hey, it's the best, and the sea views are to die for. You should come up and look.' Marcus realized what his invitation sounded like.

'Now?'

'Well, only if you want to.' He would leave it up to her. 'We can discuss whatever it is you want to talk about and have some food.'

Marcus was intending to take her to his bed. He had thought of nothing else since the day he saw her again. The decision would be hers to make. Did she want him as much as he wanted her? He was determined to find out. He hadn't felt like this about someone for so long. One-night stands had been all he was interested in, but they left him feeling as empty as when they had begun. He craved something more, but did he deserve to be loved after what he had allowed to happen to Emily?

They left the hospital room in silence, each lost in their own thoughts. Annabel kept checking over her shoulder every two minutes, which put his nerves on edge. 'So do I get a hint about what is bothering you?'

'Marcus, I really need your help. I know I haven't done anything.' She choked back her words; it had only just crossed her mind that he would say no. He couldn't, he just couldn't — the kids. She had to save the children no matter what the cost would be. 'If you can't or won't, I understand,' she added sadly.

'You're not making any sense.' He grasped her hand.

'I know, I'm sorry.' *If anyone else could hear your incoherent babble, Annabel, they would want to lock you up.*

She called the lift. A heavy aroma of disinfectant hung in the air. 'I will tell you everything, I promise.'

He squeezed her hand. 'As I recall, you saved my life, so I will help you with whatever you need.'

Relief flooded her; that was more like the old Marcus — always willing to help everyone. She had often called him selfish, but he was in fact far from it. No matter who it was, he was always one to lend a hand. A stark contrast to his playboy tag. Marcus was a very complex character. There was still sadness about him that she couldn't work out. No matter what he said, the humor and laughter he had been famous for eluded him still.

Jumping in the car, she leaned over the back seat. 'I need you to help with this,' she said, handing him the overstuffed envelope. 'Can you look? I can't work it out.'

Marcus took the envelope from her. 'Is this what you need help with?' Slowly ripping the seal, he took some of the pages. 'Accounts?'

'They're the hospital's. I don't understand it.'

Marcus looked at her, and their gazes locked for a second. 'Why don't you come for lunch at the hotel, and we will work it out together?'

'I'd like that, but . . . ' Annabel replied shyly.

'So where did you get these from?'

'Someone called me, told me to check my emails.' Annabel kept her gaze firmly attached to the road ahead. 'When I got back home, there was an email giving me the log-in details for the hospital accounts.'

She slammed her hand on the

steering wheel. 'I don't know what I'm looking for. All I know for certain is that Mr. Underwood, the chairman of the board, has no idea what has happened.' She paused for a moment to gather her thoughts. 'Mrs. Higginbottom, although she has been helpful, mentioned a third-party company for buying equipment.'

★　★　★

'Hang on, a what?' He almost shouted the words; Annabel had just piqued his interest.

'A third-party company. Apparently, it's normal practice.'

He watched as Annabel screwed her face up in confusion. 'No, Annabel, it is not normal practice.' Now he knew where to start, and he had a very good idea what was going on. This wasn't going to take long at all. He decided not to tell Annabel at least for the time being. Marcus enjoyed being in her company and didn't want it to be over just yet.

'We still on for lunch?'

'Yes, you owe me taxi fare,' she joked.

'Do I now? And what do you owe me for scaring me for life?' Marcus thought he was pushing his luck.

'Fine. I will drop you off and go home then,' she retorted.

'No, I'm sorry. I will behave.' He flashed a smile in her direction. 'At least for now,' he muttered to himself.

'Somehow, I doubt you know how to behave, Marcus Chapman.'

'Very badly,' he said, nodding in agreement.

★　★　★

They both laughed, relieving the tension that had descended. Annabel pulled up into an empty space in front of the Grand. Part of her wanted to stay in the car. The other larger part of her wanted to stay with Marcus. The feelings for him she thought had died had just curled up in her heart and slept until she saw him again.

'Look, I will come back in an hour. I've got a few things I need to do.'

Annabel didn't know how he was going to react. Would he be hurt or understand? 'Sure, but after ... ' Marcus hesitated. 'After lunch, do you want to spend the rest of the day with me?'

Annabel just stared at him before she replied in an attempt to process what he had just said. 'You've never asked me to your place before.'

'It's not that bad, is it? Well, it's not exactly my place. It's the hotel.'

'We best not.' Annabel didn't miss the hurt look on his face as she declined his offer. 'What would we do?' A hard edge laced her voice. She didn't want to admit she was scared of what would happen. They would never be able to take it back if they crossed the line.

'I just want to be with you, my Anna.' He pulled her close to him. 'I don't want to rush you into anything.' *Only down the aisle.*

'Don't hate me,' she begged, her head was telling her to run a mile, but her heart was telling her to stay with him.

Marcus lifted her chin so she looked into his eyes. 'I don't hate you. You must never think like that.'

'How about we do something else?' she suggested.

Marcus held his hands up in submission. 'Okay, okay.'

★　★　★

He usually wasn't shy with the ladies, especially when he wanted something. Marcus would make his point and very rarely get turned down by anyone of the female persuasion. The one thing he did know was his lifestyle would only end up hurting Annabel. Hiding away from the world as much as he could, not socializing — he lived in a hotel for God's sake. How was that suitable for Anna?

The strange thing was he didn't

regret what happened, just the way it did and the outcome that he never expected. A misunderstanding had torn them apart, and he so wanted to have her back in his life.

Annabel leaned over and kissed him. 'I need to see the riders. They come back today, should be at the pub in half an hour.'

'All right.' His voice was tinged with sadness.

'So, where are you taking me?' Annabel asked, desperation bleeding into her voice.

'Anywhere you want to go. The beaches for some food or you tell me.' Marcus was drowning; he had no ideas at what to do. 'We could go for a picnic on the beach; the weather seems to be holding.' He watched Annabel pull a face.

'Or if there is something you'd rather do?'

'I guess that would be okay.'

Marcus didn't miss the look on Annabel's face. No matter what he said, she still kept that stone wall around her. One minute he thought he had got through the barriers she kept erecting, and then the next, she would pull away from him.

'I will meet you back here in an hour.'

He climbed from the car and walked into the hotel.

They were very much alike, one step forward and two back. Marcus had hoped Annabel had realized by now he wasn't going to be going anywhere. He was just as scared as she was. The difference was he would never let her know.

He phoned down to reception. 'Hello, this is Mr. Chapman in room 601. I need a picnic basket.' Marcus waited for the receptionist to agree. 'All the usual picnic food.'

Receiving confirmation that his order would be ready in half an hour, Marcus then jumped in the shower and let the hot water soothe his aches and pains. He'd needed to get out of that hospital and had lied to the doctors when they asked if he was still having as much pain.

He remembered fondly the summer he had met her. The big group would go to the beach whenever the weather was nice, playing beach football or frisbee. A few of them attempted to surf but had given it up as a bad job. Marcus hoped any memories of those days would be good ones for Annabel.

He wanted to repeat all the good times they had had and forget the bad. A quick look out his hotel window would tell him if the tide was out and the elusive sand was showing. He noticed the sky looked angry. Broken gray clouds scattered the skyline, yet the sunshine broke through the cloud barrier. That was one of the good things about a seafront hotel and having the best room at the Grand — sea views. He loved to watch the waves crash against the shore. He hoped he could share it with Annabel someday.

Annabel had stayed and waited until Marcus had gone into the hotel. It had been a surreal few days. There was still an undercurrent of sexual desire between them as though they'd never been apart. Did she want that? Annabel was confused. A few kisses didn't make for a relationship.

She grabbed a CD and put it in the stereo. Dance music blared out of the speakers. It always helped her to relax and face the Spanish inquisition from Rachel. She hadn't heard from her and hoped that her friend was all right. *Had the riders known what had happened at the service station? Of course they will, Annabel, what are you thinking — you gave Marcus's bike to some bikers to take down to Land's End and back.*

No one from the ride had been in contact, and her only hope was that Rach would make it back to the finish point in one piece. No trouble, hopefully, just a smooth ride there and back, unlike her own.

Annabel was confused about Marcus. Things seemed to be going well, but she was still unsure of herself and of him. The niggly feeling she still had about him wouldn't go away. Was he still that playboy she knew? Just using her for a bit of entertainment and self-gratification? Yes, she could ask, but he would only lie to her.

The way her body betrayed her each time they were near one another; the electricity that arced between them filled the air with an atmosphere so strong you could swim through it. *Come on, Annabel, you're over-thinking things, as always.* Pulling into the Farmers Pub Lancing car park, she saw it was filling up already, the transit van with all their stuff was already there. Hers and Marcus's bags would be on it. Maybe she could claim his and take it back with her when she went out with him. She couldn't tell if his bike was there, not in the sea of almost identical bikes. Annabel would recognize his helmet first and then the bike. She couldn't be bothered to wander up and down the rows of them. So finding his would be like searching through pea soup.

Nobody hung around in the car park. Maybe they were already in the pub having a well-earned drink. Annabel looked around the pub. It was very old fashioned. Old bottles lined the shelf above the bar, and huge copper cauldrons were strategically placed around the floor. *I wouldn't want to clean those, it would take hours.* Cleaning was one job she hated the most. She looked around for her friend, finally spotting her sitting in a comfy chintz armchair next to a roaring open fire.

'Rachel,' she shouted over the din.

'Hey, Anna, where the hell have you been?' Her friend gave her an inquiring look, mixed with disapproval.

'I've been trying to get hold of you. We stopped at the first services on the route and, lucky us, got caught in a big accident.' Annabel proceeded to tell her friend what had happened. Rachel frowned and made several knowing noises whenever she mentioned Marcus, which was rather a lot.

'You weren't hurt, were you?'

Annabel caught the concern that etched her friend's face. 'No, just a scratch. Marcus came out the worst,' she replied.

'I'm glad you're okay.' Rachel patted her hand. 'Well, you missed all the fun we had. Riley tried to light a bonfire but set his leathers alight. Good job they are fireproof. Someone even got the marshmallows out and threatened to toast them on him.' Rachel let out a soft giggle. 'Then Dr. Solomon decided he would go for a swim in the sea for a bet; he didn't stay in long. Booked himself into a hotel because he had got so cold. Needed a hot bath he said. Honestly, some men are just chicken.'

Annabel wished she had been there. After all, it had all been her idea, her run. Whatever had happened would have been much more fun than what had happened to her and Marcus. The run would have given her the break she needed from work. At least Marcus's accident had moved her to take some much-needed time off, and she could spend it with him.

'We missed all your excitement then, Annabel. We didn't stop for a few hours. Everyone just kept driving.' Rachel paused. 'So, anything else you need to tell me?'

'You know that guy I was paired up with?'

'Yes?'

'Well, we have a history, sort of.'

'Go on. I'm intrigued now.'

'It was before my last year at uni. He used to hang around the pier with a group of other lads.' *God, he looked so hot in his leathers just like he does now.*

'Earth to Annabel . . . '

Embarrassed, she answered, 'Oh, I'm sorry . . . um, where was I? Oh, yes. Anyway, he always had a string of girlfriends, and I made a complete fool of myself. But he never noticed me,' Annabel said sadly. 'Not until the night before I went off to finish my medical degree. We spent a lovely night on the beach and then went back to my flat.'

Rachel had her head on her hand listening intently, Annabel wanted to laugh. Rach was always one for hot juicy gossip. 'Anyway, he spent most of the night and left before I had woken up.'

'That is just so wrong.'

She sighed. 'It was all a misunderstanding. He did leave me his number on a pizza box.'

Annabel saw Rachel's eyes widen. 'A pizza box? He left his number on a — '

'Yep, stupid, I know. We lost all those years because of it. And now I don't know if I can trust him. Would he be faithful to me, or would he cheat on me?'

'You have to give him a chance to prove himself, don't you?' encouraged Rachel.

'Yes, that's what I am doing. We're

going to spend the day together.'

'Doing what exactly?' Her friend raised her eyebrows.

'No, not that. Just enjoying each other's company. Besides, with the state Marcus is in, he isn't fit to do much except talk.' At least Annabel hoped that is all he was capable of. Yet, each time she was near him, she didn't want to just talk.

'Why don't you go then? I will grab Marcus's bag and yours and give them to you tomorrow.'

'Thanks, Rach. Oh, there is one more thing. Marcus's bike is somewhere around. Could you ask someone to take it to the Grand? If they leave the key at reception, he will get it.'

'Yeah, I will. Now, go, don't keep lover boy waiting. It's been so long since you have had a date.'

'Don't rub it in, Rach.'

Annabel hugged her friend and headed back, relieved everyone was safe. Her stomach fluttered as she thought of her plans for the rest of the day. Marcus would be waiting for her at the hotel. She had said that she didn't want to go to his room, but that was precisely what she wanted to do.

Annabel slowly drove back, trying to calm herself. A whole day with Marcus, or what was left of it. Did he know what he wanted to do, or would he be just as unsure as she was? By the time she had arrived, Marcus was waiting outside. His tight-fitting jeans accentuated his thighs. His black leather coat and white t-shirt brought the memories of that summer flooding back. It was what he had always worn. It had driven her to distraction just like it was doing now.

Annabel wasn't concentrating as she pulled into the car park and hit a lamp post as she pulled into a space. 'Damn it,' she mumbled. Jumping out, she checked for damage. Luckily, she had only dented the bumper.

'Hey, Anna, are you sure you're fit to drive?' Marcus was laughing hard. 'That hurts,' he said, clutching his ribs.

'Oh, you're so funny. Just wait,

Marcus. I will get you back for that remark.' Annabel joined in the laughter. What a klutz she was. *Anyway, it was your fault. Why do you have to look so damn hot?*

'Have you decided where you want to go?' Annabel spotted the bag in his hand.

Marcus shrugged. 'I thought we could go on the beach and have a picnic like the old days.'

Annabel winced. Did she want to recreate the old days? Maybe it wouldn't be too bad. What could possibly go wrong? She could lose her heart, or lose her friend, but she had already lost the former. 'Why don't we drive down to Madera drive, go to that part of the beach? If it gets too hard for you, there's that little café. They do great homemade cakes and lattes.'

8

'Sounds like a plan to me,' Marcus replied as he climbed into Annabel's car. He had a sudden urge to build a sand castle. How good would that be? With his ribs the way they were, he wasn't sure, and he had no tools. He planned on acting like a big kid and taking Annabel along for the ride.

It had been so long since he had played in the sand. The last time had been with Emily. She would have loved Annabel, and he got the feeling that Annabel had wanted children but for some reason had never had them. For the short time he had been in hospital, Marcus realized that he could no longer live in the past. Life was precious, and he had wasted enough time wishing he could change something that could never be changed. No amount of what-if's would bring his darling daughter back. She would be forever ingrained in his heart and mind.

He looked over at Anna and saw her filling her pockets with pebbles and shells. He saw it as an excuse to act like a child and get away with it.

'What are you doing, Anna?'

'I'm collecting pebbles and shells. I am going to decorate an old box I found in a charity shop. Upcycling relaxes me.'

He loved the childish smile on her face; this was more like the old Annabel. He was sure she was a Peter Pan-style girl. Why had she hidden her true self away? *Come on, Marcus, that is exactly what you have been doing for a year.* Then he had an idea, and there was no way Annabel could beat him. 'Hey, Anna, how about a sand-castle-building competition before we eat?'

He waited for a response as she mulled over his proposition.

'I can see this costing me something.'

'Oh, you know me too well.' He

chuckled. 'Whoever loses buys the lattes. Deal?'

'That's a lot less than what I was expecting.'

Marcus loved that they were getting along so well. A wave of guilt washed over him. He still hadn't told her about Emily or Josie. Not that Josie mattered. After all, he had only been married a few months before she left him.

'Marcus, are you okay?'

'Er, yeah. I'm good.' Had Anna noticed? Would she question him further? Marcus needed a change of topic. He couldn't tell her, not yet. He didn't want to ruin the day he was having by talking about sad things.

'I will just go and buy the buckets and spades.' Marcus wandered over to a stall on the promenade that had all sorts of different-sized buckets, some shaped as castles, while others were plain. Considering his options for a few moments, he decided to get two different-shaped ones. The colors didn't matter. As soon as they had done, he would give them to some child to use. Once he had beaten his Anna. He debated on telling her he had won a sand-castle-building competition in his youth. *That's a laugh. You and Emily won it.* Marcus liked being sneaky, and his underhanded tactics were working.

He handed Annabel the castle-shaped one. 'Whoever makes the biggest and best sand castle construction wins.'

'Really? I think I'm about to get hustled.' Her brow knitted together. 'How many times have you done this?' Annabel asked.

'I may have made a few in the past.' He hastily added, 'Not for years, though.'

Don't look at my eyes. She might see the glint of mischief he knew would be there.

'Admit it, Marcus. You still like to play on the beach yourself. This isn't just a bet,' she chided.

Marcus tried to laugh, but it hurt too much to let out a huge belly laugh. 'You know me too well. Give me any excuse to be a kid again, and I will take it.'

It was nice to be here with Anna, no worries, no clients vying for his advice. Just the two of them having some old-fashioned fun with no cares in the world, even if he did have an unfair advantage. They walked away from each other and started building their own creations. Marcus wasn't getting too far. He loved how the light bounced off Anna's raven-colored hair, bathing her in a golden halo. But as he looked up at the sky, dark ominous clouds blew over.

'You haven't finished yet?' he shouted over. Sand flew in all directions as he started building. Damp sand was always the best. That was one little secret he was going to keep to himself. Marcus wanted to laugh out loud as he caught Anna struggling with her building.

'Now, now, don't talk to me. I'm busy!' Her voice rose a little with irritation.

I best leave her alone. Marcus put the final touches to his — a few shells and pebbles as decoration. He watched as Anna tipped the latest sand castle over, it collapsed immediately. Marcus wanted to laugh, to make fun out of her but decided that he better keep quiet. He was having so much fun, but the pain was increasing in his side. It wouldn't be long before he had to stop and sit down.

'Any excuse, just admit I won.'

'No, you would love that wouldn't you.' A groan escaped her lips as another sand castle came out all wrong and partially collapsed.

He had finished his creation and sat on the beach clutching his ribs. The toothed monster was back much more ferocious than ever, but he wanted a picnic with her. Marcus didn't want to leave; not yet when the day had only just begun.

*   *   *

Annabel threw her spade and bucket down. 'Okay, I give in. You win.' The one thing she hated most was being beaten by anyone. *Oh, you will pay, Marcus. Don't you worry about that.* But it had been the most fun she had had in years. 'Best go buy you that latte.'

'Yes, you had,' he agreed.

Annabel walked back over to him and held out her hand. Marcus struggled to his feet using her as an anchor. She leaned toward him brushing her lips softly against his. His hands wrapped around her waist and pulled her gently into him. Her whole body responded to him as she hungrily searched entrance to his mouth. Marcus seemed to be playing it cool, frustrating the flames of passion that had ignited. She wanted him, needed him to fulfill her every fantasy, to make her feel wanted and loved. His hesitation scared Annabel. Was there something wrong with her? Did he see this as a game? Annabel didn't want to think so badly of Marcus, but he was leaving her with a sinking feeling in the pit of her stomach.

Annabel pulled away. 'Let's go get that latte.'

'Hey, baby, what's wrong?' Marcus kept a tight hold on her. 'You're not going till you tell me.'

Annabel bit her bottom lip, she couldn't face him. Instead, she looked at the sand. 'This isn't a game, is it?' She hesitated. 'I mean us. I don't even know what's happening. A few days ago we were barely talking, and now we're like this.'

She hadn't wanted to say any of it but knew he wouldn't stop the loving bone-crushing hug until she did.

'Oh, baby, I don't play games like that. Not now. I want to be with you.'

She looked deep into his eyes, losing herself for a moment in the warmth shining there. Had she read into things too much? Had the playboy actually grown up? Something in his demeanor screamed out to her that it was the closest she was going to get to an answer. Marcus still held back.

'Lattes.' It was all she said, but Annabel had to give herself breathing space. She had to think about anything rather than how she really wanted to be in his bed. Anger boiled up inside of her. How could her heart and body betray her? Hadn't they been there before? Didn't they remember where that had gotten them?

★ ★ ★

'Sure, come on.' Marcus reluctantly loosened his grip on her. Did Annabel really have such a low opinion of him? 'I will even let you buy me a cake.'

'What about the picnic stuff?'

Lifting the bag up, he said, 'We could always have it in a while.' He locked fingers with her squeezing tightly.

Marcus wanted to know what Annabel was really thinking, what she was holding back. A vivid picture of Annabel and Emily walking hand in hand along the beach popped into his head. The feeling of being run over by a steamroller hit him square in the chest. The woman next to him had been his future until that fateful night. How could he have let go so easily? Being a bad boy was one thing as long as he hadn't hurt his friends, but he hadn't given consideration to anyone else then. He'd once set fire to someone's beach hut at a barbecue; they had all been too drunk to care — laughing as someone's possessions went up in flames. He cringed at that now and all the other not-quite-legal stuff he had done.

Breaking the speed limit on his bike was par for the course in those days, to hell with the consequences of anything. He was trying to make it up to her in whatever way he could. Marcus would give anything to make her happy, to make them both happy. Yet, Annabel always seemed to back off. Time would tell how serious things would get if his Anna would allow it. Ever since that day at the car park, he had not thought about anything other than making Anna happy and protecting her at any cost.

'Marcus, you're not in pain, are you?'

He caught the worry in her voice. 'A little. These jeans are hurting me.' The bruising had reached his stomach, making even the smallest movements painful. 'Forever the doctor, my Anna.'

'Sorry, bad habit.'

Marcus laughed. 'No, not a bad habit at all. It shows just how much you care for people.' It was a rare trait but one that had shone in Annabel since he had first set eyes on her. She had been so unlike the other girls he knew, who made it quite clear that they were available. Annabel had watched him from a distance. He wasn't blind to the fact she liked him. Her quiet fascination had soon become his. He wanted her, but Marcus had also wanted to protect her from himself. She wasn't a girl he ever wanted to hurt. Something niggled inside him. That was precisely what he was doing. Just as Anna protected her patients, he would protect her from himself. He didn't want to walk away, but he would if it meant he didn't break her heart.

Shells crunched under their feet as they walked in silence to the café, looking up at the angry black clouds swirling in the sky. 'It looks like it's going to rain,' he said, releasing her hand to grasp the picnic bag in that hand.

'Let's get a coffee, and then I will get you back. It won't do you any good.' She hesitated. 'To get even more ill.'

By the time they had reached the café, small drops of rain began to fall, tinkling off the metal tables. 'We could go inside?' Annabel suggested.

'No, let's sit out here. I don't get enough fresh air as it is.' *Admit it, man, you spend all your time in the office or your hotel room. You live like a hermit and have no real friends.*

Complying with his demands, she still ordered him around. 'Sit down. I will go and get the drinks.'

Annabel walked off leaving him to

watch the waves as they swirled and crashed against the shore. Disappointment crept in as it looked like their beach picnic would be postponed for another day. The wind was picking up, sending sand everywhere. He wanted to suggest they take the picnic to his room. They could have a carpet picnic like he and Emily used to have. Confusion warred with desire, leaving him at a loss as to what to do. How could he prove that it wasn't a game, even though he was so unsure of everything himself?

Marcus breathed heavily. This was turning into a very strange day. There was so much he wanted to say, but so much he had to conceal. Annabel had in a very short time broken down the many barriers he had built. The past still haunted them both. His still raw and unyielding, but just seeing Anna smiling and happy would be enough. He wasn't sure he would ever see either.

Interrupting his thoughts, she came

out of the café with two steaming latte mugs.

'Here you go. I'll just go get the cakes.' Placing the cups on the table, she dashed back inside.

The spots of rain were getting heavier. 'Please don't rain, not yet,' he mumbled, staring up at the sky. They'd parked the car a fair distance away from the café where he would usually park. If it was going to rain, let it be when he was in the car nice and protected.

'Here, Marcus. I got you a big cream cake. Thought you could do with something nice after the hospital food.'

'It wasn't great. I can think of much nicer things.'

He loved how a blush crept up into Annabel's face. 'I bet you do. Drink your latte.'

Had she really not thought about it? He laced his fingers around his coffee cup and held it near his mouth letting the strong aroma fill his senses. 'So do I get to take you out for dinner?' He came across as rather abrupt and checked himself. 'You could pick anywhere you want.'

'Not tonight. Besides, I only broke you out of the hospital a few hours ago,' she said, shaking her head. 'Give yourself time to heal.'

Marcus caught her eyes narrowing. He put his cup down, running his hands through his hair in frustration. *See? There she goes again, backing away.* 'Look, truth be told, I'm really enjoying being here with you and . . . '

'And?' she repeated.

'I don't want the day to end, not yet,' Marcus said. He was enjoying himself too much for the first time in a long time.

'I'm not going anywhere till you've shared your picnic with me.' Placing her drink down, she added, 'You hustled me over there, didn't you?'

Marcus tried to put on his most innocent face. 'Whatever do you mean?'

'The sand castle thing, you've done it before.' She looked so cute when her brows knitted together.

'Er, okay, okay, it's a fair cop, your honor.' He held up his hands.

'That sounded like such a cliché, Marcus, honestly.' Annabel laughed. 'So tell me. Or you can't have your cake.' With that, she promptly picked up his plate and moved it onto the empty table behind her.

'No, where is the fairness in that?' Marcus grinned.

'I don't know. You tell me how much you cheated.'

'Fine, can I have my cake then?' He was beginning to get very hungry. 'I won a sand-castle-building competition last year with E — with Eric, an employee of mine. Team building, that sort of thing.' He let out a long slow breath. He had just nearly ruined everything. No, Emily could never ruin anything. It was Annabel's reaction he was afraid of. The longer he kept it from her, the harder it was going to be to tell the whole story. Perhaps he should have said something on the first day.

'So I was hustled and made to buy the coffee. If we go out again, it will be your turn.'

'Will it now?' Marcus kept quiet. His mind raced in several different directions, but one thing was perfectly clear. They were both enjoying each other's company. 'Where's my bike?' He had forgotten all about it for a while.

'Rachel is going to get it brought to the hotel. It might even be there when you go back, along with your bag.' She took a sip of her latte. 'Why motorbikes?'

'Now there's a question. The freedom, the wind blowing your troubles away, at least for a short while.' He always became animated when he discussed bikes.

'I think they're dangerous.'

'So you still don't like them?' he said, drinking the last dregs of coffee from his cup.

'I just think they are so dangerous. You don't know how many bikers come into the hospital to be patched up.'

'Not everyone is a bad rider, and it isn't always our fault.' He patted her hand.

'I guess not,' she conceded. Why did Marcus have to be right about what he was saying? A lot of the time bikers were injured through the actions of other motorists.

The rain that had threatened to come and spoil their day came down heavily without much warning. The little drops of rain hadn't been a bother, but now it was sending people rushing in all directions, hunting for cover. There was no way he could run for cover. He hurt too much. The sand castle building had seen to that. Bending over had caused him a great deal of discomfort, and like an idiot, he had left his pills in the hotel.

Even the short walk to the beach had been too much for him, but Marcus didn't want to admit that to Annabel. He was having too much fun being with her, and he wasn't going to let a little thing like pain stop him. They walked slowly, by the time they had reached the car, rain was pouring out of their shoes.

'Great,' Annabel said. 'I'll drop you back at the hotel and head home to dry out.'

A few minutes later, they parked back outside the Grand. 'The hotel may just give you a season ticket to their car park. You've been here three times today.' He chuckled.

'Here, I'll help you into the hotel,' Annabel said. 'Come on.'

Marcus climbed gingerly out of the car, his movements cautious and unsure. Annabel entered the hotel lobby with him. The staff wandered here, there, and everywhere, their black and purple uniforms immaculately pressed.

'Annabel, do you want to come up? It may take you a while before you get home. I don't want you to catch cold.' Marcus moved toward her slowly, this time he was going to be with her. For days he had thought of nothing more than making love to her, about making her his.

'I best go, Marcus. You need to rest.'
Marcus spoke so low, it was almost a growl. 'Is that what the doctor orders?'

★ ★ ★

'Yes, she does.' She leaned forward and kissed him on the cheek. His loving gaze made her legs weak. The caress of his hand down her cheek sent frissons of passion soaring through her body. 'I will see you later.'

'How about you just come up for five minutes,' Marcus pleaded. 'It's my turn to need your help with something.'

Annabel looked around quickly to see if anyone was paying attention to their little game. 'Oh, do you now?'

'Come on. We can't stay in the hotel reception all day.' Taking her hand, he kissed it gently, sending shivers up and down her spine. It was such a gentle gesture, Annabel couldn't think straight. They had spent such a great day together; it was too early to end yet.

9

Marcus walked toward the lift, and Annabel followed slightly behind him as she tried to get her emotions under control. Her heart raced, and the hairs on her arms stood on end. She didn't want them to just have dinner; it had been nice lying on the bed with him at the hospital. Listening to his gentle snoring had lulled her into slumber. They had fit together so perfectly until that stupid nurse had ruined it.

'Marcus, how come you like looking out to sea?'

'Because the sea can be an angry mother bear looking after its young, or calm and soothing like classical music.'

'Very poetic.' The memory hit her so fast she had almost forgotten.

That summer they had all gone down to the beach for one last barbecue. She sat on the pebbled beach holding

Marcus's hand. It was like all her dreams had come true. Marcus was finally there just for her. No more girls vied for his attention; it was just the two of them. Everyone else played football or Frisbee or just sat huddled around the blazing driftwood fire.

'What are you smiling at?'

'Nothing, I just remembered something.' She cast her eyes to the floor, and heat filled her cheeks. She wasn't ready to share her memory.

'That's the first smile you've given me today.'

'I resent that. I smiled at you on the beach.' Annabel gave herself a mental shake; she had begun to over-think things. *Just because you've shared a few kisses doesn't mean that he wants anything else. He could just be being friendly.* 'I just — '

'Don't feel like it today,' Marcus added. 'No.'

Annabel turned her face to his. Those blue-gray eyes mesmerized her, and Marcus hadn't lost the ability to leave her heart thumping and feeling very much like a teenager on a first date, with just one glance. No wonder all the girls fell for him, with his silky smooth voice, toned ass, and those eyes — the sort you want to lose yourself in and never break free.

★   ★   ★

Marcus used his keycard to unlock the door. He was feeling more and more uncomfortable in his tight jeans and t-shirt. He needed to put on something looser and relax his body. The painkillers he had received at the hospital were just wearing off, and the dull throbbing was becoming a saber-toothed tiger.

He caught Annabel looking around his room. 'I know it's messy.'

'And you complained about my flat?' Annabel chided.

'I don't want a lecture. It was wrong of me. It caused me to . . . ' Marcus didn't finish, at least not out loud. He couldn't admit that he was falling hard for Annabel. They were playing a game, each one as unsure as the other. He had a lot to prove to her. If helping to save the children's ward was what he had to do, so be it. He would even fund it himself, if necessary.

The soft furnishings left a lot to be desired; old-fashioned chintz patterns adorned everything, and the small settee in front of the bed was extremely uncomfortable. It was such a waste of time. He really needed to find a flat, a house, anything. Living here was beginning to get to him.

'What's wrong?' Concern etched her voice.

'I don't suppose you fancy helping me look for a better place to live than this?' Marcus moved his hand in a sweeping gesture.

'Sure, we could have a look around tomorrow, if you have time.'

'I have to go into the office, but we could grab some sales forms.'

'Okay, I will meet you somewhere.'

Marcus grasped her wrist. 'No, please

come with me. There's someone I'd like you to meet.'

He caught the horrified look that flashed across her face. 'There's no need to worry.' He laughed out loud. 'It's only my secretary.'

'Oh . . . '

'She is old enough to be my mother and used to change my nappies.'

'Right, I guess I jumped to conclusions.'

Had that been a bit of jealousy on Annabel's part? Marcus wasn't going to ask her as that would cause her more embarrassment. Did she really think that little of him? A secret smile crossed his lips. Marcus was glad he had found her again.

If they hadn't wasted so much time being apart — *No, no, Marcus, that's not what you should be thinking.* Annabel had left him, but she was back now, filling the gaping hole of grief and sadness with happiness. Marcus never thought he would be able to feel so much joy again. Amazing how a small bit of generosity could reap such rewards. Marcus made a vow to himself that he would treat Annabel to a nice meal. All her selfless hard work would pay off.

These bloody jeans. He winced as the waistband felt tighter than ever. 'Annabel, would you . . . um . . . could you?'

'Could I what, Marcus?'

Marcus thought for a moment on how to phrase what he wanted to say without upsetting her. 'These jeans are hurting me. Could you help me into something looser?'

He waited for a response. Marcus hated being reliant on anybody. He always did everything for himself, even when he had been younger. 'It's nothing you haven't seen before.' *Why did I just say that?* 'As a doctor, I mean,' he quickly added. 'I thought — I mean — ' *Marcus, you sound like a child, man up.*

'I knew what you meant.' Annabel's hearty laugh resonated around the room. 'I was only teasing you.'

He let out a breath he didn't know he was holding.

171

Annabel walked tentatively toward him; he had wanted her to touch him, to see him. To run her hands over his body, Marcus just stood there and gazed at her. Were the same thoughts running through her head as were running through his? Carefully, Annabel took his arms out of his t-shirt without his having to stretch too far and then pulled it over his head.

★ ★ ★

Her gaze never left his. She placed her hands on his chest, moving them slowly downward toward his scar. Marcus brushed his hands down her arm, sending her already jangling nerves into free fall.

'I didn't mean . . . '

Annabel knew it had been her job to make him better, to save him, just as he was saving her from loneliness. Friends were all right, but they couldn't be there for her all the time. When her house felt too empty, her movements sent echoes bouncing off its walls. The past few days with Marcus had been the happiest she had felt for a long time, even though they had been eventful, it wasn't over yet.

'I know, my Anna.'

Marcus's voice was soft and hypnotic.

Pulling her toward him, he held her close, and Annabel rested her head on his chest. The sound of his heart pounding in his chest was soothing and matched her own erratic heartbeat.

'I thought you needed my help?' Pulling away slightly, she brushed her hands down his hard muscular chest and proceeded to undo his belt. Sliding his jeans to the floor, Annabel felt Marcus leaning against her so she could remove them fully.

★　★　★

Later, Annabel savored the feeling of satisfaction he left her with. His breath was warm and moist against her face.

173

Her heart raced.

'Come here, Anna,' Marcus said, pulling her into his strong embrace, their bodies molding to each other perfectly.

'I can't believe that,' she replied breathlessly.

'What? That making love could be so . . . ' Marcus added.

'Yes.' Annabel still hadn't come down from the cloud Marcus had taken her to. She had given herself happily to him, and she knew she was falling in love with him again. Annabel made a silent vow not to tell him. She would take today as what it had been — a sweet, wonderful moment full of the feelings they had obviously kept for each other. A tear rolled silently down her face, but she quickly wiped it away.

'Anna, do you want to do anything tomorrow night?'

'Like what?' She turned to face him, moving her arm lazily over his side.

'A meal out anywhere you want.'

Moving her mouth from side to side

as she thought about where to go. 'Leon's.'

'Leon's?' he asked questioningly.

'It's a new place in town. Everyone who's anyone goes.' Annabel was animated.

'Well, we can go there. How about I pick you up at eight tomorrow? I will call them about a reservation.'

* * *

He looked at Anna, but she had given in to exhaustion with a sweet serene look etched on her face. Marcus kissed the top of her head and the tip of her nose, holding her tightly. He felt like such a cad. He was always so careful, but the last thing he had thought about with his Anna was having safe sex.

He shouldn't have made love to her. Not because he didn't want to, but the pain he was now in was excruciating. Marcus needed to get up and take his tablets, but he didn't want to move, not yet. He liked having Annabel close to him, her hot breath on his face, and the feel of her heart beating against his chest.

Marcus lay for a while until it was too painful for him to stay still any longer and carefully eased out of bed. He stood and stared lovingly down on Annabel's sleeping form. He pulled his side of the duvet over her to prevent her getting cold. *Now, my tablets and those accounts. I can bear the uncomfortable sofa to work on and let her sleep. If I need to make calls, I will go down to reception. Sounds like a plan.*

He set about taking his medication and then grabbed the printed pages, a notebook, and a calculator. He started to go through the accounts; it was easy enough with the information Annabel had provided. Marcus looked down the lists for all the equipment purchased and the names of machinery. There had been six MRI scan machines bought in the past two years. Strange, Oakwood hospital wasn't that large.

After an hour, he had all the figures

he needed. It added up to several million pounds. Though some of the equipment was obviously needed, others were overkill or redundant, which meant that money was siphoned off directly into someone's pockets, but who?

How stupid had he been? There was only one person it could have been — Mrs. Higginbottom herself. Of all the low-down, dirty tricks. 'Damn it.' Marcus realized how loud he had been and quickly turned to check that Annabel remained sleeping.

Marcus looked around the room for some clothes. He should really phone the police or someone, but he didn't want to ruin his day with Annabel. Hospital politics is what she had said. It was more than that; it was fraud. Whoever else was involved was going down. No, he'd have a shower first, perhaps a cold one. Staring down at Anna's naked form in his bed was sending him over the edge, and he would make damn sure he was taking her with him. How could someone he had only just become reacquainted with stoke the flames of passion in him more than any other woman?

★ ★ ★

Annabel reached out a hand, feeling the bed next to her. It was empty. Would Marcus leave her again? Sitting up, she pulled her knees to her chest holding her legs tightly. A tear fell onto the duvet. Why had he left her again? She cursed him quietly so as not to disturb the people in the rooms next to his. He hadn't changed. She felt used and unloved. Once, just once, she had wanted Marcus to feel the way she did. To love her the way she desperately loved him. No, people like Marcus only cared about one thing.

'Did you call, Anna?' Marcus's voice called from behind the bathroom door.

'You didn't leave?' she stuttered.

'Of course not. What did you think I had done?'

Annabel looked down at the duvet and played with the sheet. 'I thought you had left me like you did the last time.'

'First, this is my hotel room. Second, I didn't mean to leave you that day.' Marcus sighed heavily. 'Do we need to go over this again?'

Annabel stayed silent. She knew Marcus was angry, and the last thing she wanted to do was make him angrier. 'I guess not.'

'Stay with me today,' Marcus implored. He leaned over and kissed her forehead. He was doing a bad job of trying to ignore the pain; after all, there was nothing he could do. He should know it would heal itself when it was good and ready.

'What, you want me to be with you?' Annabel looked puzzled. Even though she had woken in his bed, she couldn't shake the feeling she had been just another conquest.

'Yes, of course.' Marcus stood with a towel wrapped around his waist.

Annabel found it very difficult to pay attention to what he was telling her. Drinking in the sight of him, she wanted him to come back to bed. Her worries seemed to disappear when he was lying next to her.

She wasn't sure what to say. 'To do what?'

'Anything. To be honest, I'd not given it much thought. I just know I don't want you to leave.'

★　★　★

'I need to go into the office for about an hour, but after that we could do anything you want to.' Marcus thought about the huge pile of paperwork he still had to do and the accounts for Greg. It really was a good thing the tax year wasn't coming to an end just yet. 'You did say you would help me look for a house.'

'Sure, I'd forgotten about that. I'd like to see where you work.'

'So come to work with me for a while?'

Marcus wanted to punch the air with joy but thought better of it. Even though he had asked Anna to stay with him, he hadn't expected her to say yes.

'If you want, tonight, we could go to that restaurant you mentioned. I will reserve a table.'

'There is absolutely no way you can get a table on such short notice.'

Marcus laughed loudly. 'When you have money, my dear, you can get in anywhere.'

'Okay, Mr. Flashy.' She didn't like the thought of Marcus flashing his cash around when so many others were struggling or in need. Being who he was, he would do what he wanted, and the consequences could go hang.

'Humph, and here I thought I was your bad boy biker.'

Annabel put her head in her hands. 'Don't repeat that stupid nickname. I'm surprised you even remembered it.'

'You would be surprised at what I can remember.' Marcus moved with stealth, swiftly removed his towel, and kissed her hungrily as his hands caressed her body.

'Marcus — '

'Shh, baby, I need you.' He grasped her hair in his hands. He had needed this connection since he'd climbed from the bed last night.

★ ★ ★

Their breathing was ragged as they lay entwined in each other's arms. 'Good morning, sweets.'

'Morning,' she replied, holding him tighter. Annabel couldn't help but smile. A stark contrast to how she felt when she'd first woke up.

'You happy?'

'Yes, you know I am.' Did she dare tell him she was still worried about everything? The sinking feeling she had earlier was still as strong as ever. Annabel didn't think, didn't know if they had a future.

No, Marcus would never settle down.

This was all she would ever be, someone he could have for a bit of fun whenever he pleased. He was still a playboy but a playboy with a lot more money than he had before.

'What's wrong, Anna?'

She caught the concern in his voice. 'Nothing, I've just been thinking about what you said about going to work with you.' She ran his hands over his chest. 'I'm not sure it's a good idea. It's like meeting your parents.'

'Oh, come on. It's nothing like meeting my parents. It's just work.'

Annabel wasn't so sure about meeting his employees. How the hell was he going to introduce her? As his latest fling? She had more important things to think about, like the hospital. There were only three more days of her holiday left.

'Look, if you're that concerned, then you could stay with Mary.'

'I'd rather just stay here?'

'Anna, come on, let's go. It won't take long. Let me just go get all the paperwork, and we can come back here.'

Reluctantly, she got dressed and walked out of the hotel with him. When the valet brought the car around, they sped off to his office.

Annabel started imagining a young blonde woman with legs to die for. The image stayed in her head all the way to the office. Why was she getting so jealous? There was absolutely no point, no point to any of it. Anger bubbled up inside of her. She had been so happy this morning, and now she was letting her thoughts get the better of her. Too lost in their thoughts to speak, Annabel was frightened that she had just given her heart away.

Marcus held open the office door to reveal an elderly lady at the reception desk with her white hair tied back in a ponytail.

'Annabel, this is Mary, my secretary. Is it okay if I leave you in her capable hands?'

Annabel was relieved that she wasn't

what the young good-looking girl she had thought. Marcus winked at her and swept a brief kiss across her cheek.

'Go on, Marcus. Those papers need signing,' Mary piped up. She stood and shook Annabel's hand. 'Come get a cup of tea with me.

Annabel stared around the reception. Huge comfy leather seats lined the walls, and a copy of Monet's *Water Lilies* hung above the oak reception desk. The office was clean but very masculine in its colors and textures.

'Oh, he is very much a man's man. I have tried to get him to add color to the place, but he won't.' Mary indicated the kitchen area. 'If he could, he would have had his bike in here to sit on.'

'Yes, he always was mad on the things. I have never understood why,' Annabel replied in agreement.

Over a cup of tea, she and Mary discussed everything from the weather to cooking, even her job. The old lady seemed to care a great deal about Marcus. It was nice to know he had someone keeping an eye on him. Annabel had discovered his parents lived in Spain, so he was quite alone here, apart from friends and his old neighbor.

Just as they were about to have another cup of tea, Marcus reappeared with a thunderous look on his face. 'Anna, could we postpone the house search?'

'Sure, what's wrong?' *Here we go. He doesn't want to spend any more time with me.*

'Don't look like that,' he replied.

Annabel didn't think she had pulled a face. 'I'm not, I mean . . . '

'The accounts I need to do are a real mess. I thought I could get it done in an hour.'

Annabel let out a breath she didn't know she'd been holding. 'Sure. Here's my address.'

'Don't worry, my dear. I will look after him. Marcus, stop acting like a petulant child and sort whatever it is you need to sort out.'

'Mary, I'm not. Anna, see you later. I will get you a car.'

Marcus grabbed hold of her, pulled her close, and kissed her hard.

'Go, get your work done.' Annabel kissed him goodbye and headed for the door.

She heard Mary's stern voice as she was walking to the door. 'Have you told her, Marcus?'

Annabel walked quickly out the door. He was married. What else could she have meant? *No, I'm being silly. He cares about me, I think.*

10

Annabel had come straight home from his office and now stood in her bedroom rifling through her clothes, although there seemed to be more clothes on her bed than in her wardrobe. Marcus was picking her up in half an hour, and she wasn't anywhere near ready. She had no idea what to wear and felt as though she was going out on a first date. Picking out a black dress with plunging neckline and low-cut back, she smiled.

'This will do.' Her stomach flipped. They had been seeing each other for a while, but a niggling doubt kept creeping into her head. She had never seen his home. He didn't seem to want her there; if they spent the night together, it was usually at her house or the hotel.

Dressing quickly, she applied just a

bit of makeup — enough to cover the fact she had done quite a few double shifts recently. Annabel made her mind up to confront Marcus about the sleeping arrangements; it was just too strange he hadn't allowed her in his home.

It hadn't been hard to find out where he lived. The Internet was a wealth of information. Annabel chuckled to herself; she sounded like a stalker all because she wanted to know what he was hiding. One night after work, she drove out to his home, but it was in total darkness. No car parked on the driveway, and the garden was overgrown, so much so that if she stood in the middle of the lawn she would have virtually disappeared.

The doorbell rang, interrupting her thoughts. Grabbing her handbag, Annabel rushed downstairs. The giddy schoolgirl feelings still hadn't disappeared. The honeymoon period was still very much alive in their relationship. Opening the door wide, Marcus stood with a huge bunch of roses and baby's breath adding a splash of coolness to them.

'Here you go, darling.' Marcus handed her the bouquet and brushed his lips tenderly over hers.

'They're beautiful. Thank you.' He was so sweet, maybe if they hadn't had that misunderstanding so many years ago — *No, Annabel, at least you're together now.* 'Come in, I'll just put these in water.'

'Sure, but come here first.'

Marcus pulled her to him and hungrily claimed her mouth, his tongue searching for entrance. Wrapping his fingers through her hair, he pulled her closer. The bouquet fell from her grasp onto the tiled stone floor. Putting her arms around his waist, she held Marcus so tightly, not wanting to let go. Annabel's whole body responded to him. They fit so perfectly together. Her skin burned at his touch. A white heat filled her belly as electricity arched between them.

Before Annabel lost all coherent thought, she reluctantly pulled away. 'We're going to be late if we carry on like this.'

★ ★ ★

'I can think of better things to do than go out for a meal,' Marcus complained. He was just beginning to enjoy himself. He was trying to put off what he should have told Anna from the beginning.

'I can think of much better things too.'

Marcus loved the little glint in her eye.

'But it's so hard to get a table at Leon's. I really want to see what the fuss is all about, Marcus. Come on.'

Marcus let out a breath. 'Okay, okay, you win.' He released his grip on her. Well, this meal would go one of two ways — by the end of the night, he would still have Annabel by his side or he wouldn't. He bent down and picked up the flowers. 'Don't these need water?' he reminded her.

Marcus gave the flowers back to her and watched as she dashed to the kitchen. 'Just give me two minutes.'

Marcus waited. The atmosphere had changed between them. Or was he just overthinking the situation? He hoped she wouldn't walk out of his life again, but there would be nothing he could do if she did.

As quickly as she had gone, she reappeared. 'Come on.' Grasping her hand, Marcus smiled down at her. For the first time in a long time, he was happy. He never wanted this to end.

They drove the short distance to Leon's, a posh new restaurant that had just opened up in Brighton. With its marble pillars and clean lines, the restaurant was more suited to Beverly Hills in America than a south coast town. But celebrities traveled down from London for the Michelin-starred cuisine.

Handing his keys to the valet to park his car around the back of Leon's,

Marcus turned and reached for Annabel's hand.

'It looks so busy,' Annabel commented, looking at the huge line in front of the building and snaking around the corner. 'Wonder if we need to queue up.'

'No, Anna, trust me.'

He caught the look of pain that flashed across her face. She still didn't trust him. A sharp pain stabbed at his heart. He had done everything he could to make things up to her. He was at a loss as to what to do next, and his news tonight would definitely make things worse between them, not better.

Marcus walked to the front of the line. 'Excuse me, we have a table booked.' Marcus used his most authoritative voice.

'Name.' The concierge was dressed head to foot in black and carried a clipboard.

'Chapman, and it's a table for two.'

The man briefly looked at his clipboard before saying. 'Yes, go on through.'

'That's so strange, Marcus.'

'What's strange, Anna?'

Annabel looked back and indicated with her head. 'Well, imagine having a clipboard with all the reservations on it. The places I go to eat are usually pubs and all-night cafés.'

'I guess all those people in line want to get in.' Marcus wasn't sure, and he didn't really care as long as Anna got into the restaurant. Everyone else could go hang. Nothing would ever be too much for her.

It was as nice as all the reviews said it was. Most of the staff were dressed in black with a few of the wine waiters in red as they carried carafes of expensive wine around the room.

'Oh, Marcus, it looks so beautiful in here. I wonder if the food will taste as good?'

'I hope so, sweets. I really hope so for the price it's going to cost.' Money wasn't any object for him, but he hated wasting it on something that wasn't worth it, like horrid meals.

They were shown to their table and handed menus with total efficiency. If Marcus didn't know better, he would think they were robots. Here you are, sir, thank you, sir. The waiters and waitresses could simper and smirk to whomever they wanted, but it was rather overdone for his liking. A few moments later, with equal efficiency, their orders were taken. Leon's was a well-oiled machine, and one thing done out of order would throw things off balance.

'Why did you want to come here?' Marcus asked her curiously.

'Well, most of the neurosurgeons have been, and all say it's wonderful.' Annabel looked at the table before she continued. 'I guess I was a little jealous that they could afford to come and I couldn't.'

'You make a fair point, but I think you could have afforded it.' Marcus eyed the prices in the menu. Definitely not cheap, but far from being unafford-able. Maybe Anna had better things to spend her money on than nights out or just no one to go out with.

'Hey, normal doctors don't make that much, you know?' The hurt in her voice was unmistakable.

Just as Marcus was going to start telling her his story, the waitress brought around their starter, interrupting his flow.

'Are you going to tell me how a millionaire playboy hasn't been here before?' Her face filled with curiosity.

'Anna, it has never appealed to me. I have seen so many people make money and then lose it in bad investments that I don't see the point in wasting my own.' Marcus closed his eyes for a moment. 'Listen, sweets, we need to talk.'

'Oh, yes, I know. I haven't told you what the board has done, have I?'

'Er, no, I don't remember you saying anything.'

His beautiful woman was like a school kid. 'They've agreed to keep the children's ward open for another year.

With all the money raised, it pays for the running costs.'

'That's great, but what happens to the children's ward after a year?' Marcus picked up his pâté and took a small bite. Adding silently, *they will never shut it by the time I have finished.*

'Well, there won't be any money left.' She sighed heavily. 'The board has spare to keep the ward open for about a month after the initial year.

'If we can repeat the ride and gain the sort of sponsorship we did this time, I hope the funds raised can keep it open another year. Did I tell you we received several generous anonymous donations?' Annabel grew animated as she talked about the job she loved.

'No, you didn't.' Marcus was glad she hadn't figured out the largest donation had come from him.

'I'm so glad it isn't going to shut — '

Marcus placed his hand on hers. 'Do you know how beautiful you look?'

'Marcus, behave. We're out for a meal.'

The blush, which now crept endearingly over her face, told Marcus a different story. By the time dessert came, he had had enough of the restaurant. He just wanted to take Annabel home and show her just how much she meant to him.

'So, what did you want to tell me?'

Damn. He had forgotten about that. He was enjoying staring lovingly at her face. In one moment, Annabel had ruined any thoughts he had about making love to her. There was no way she would want him after this. No, he wasn't going to let her go, not now that he had her back. Why the hell did he sound like a little school boy and not a man? 'I haven't told you this, and you may get angry.'

'Marcus, how bad could it be?'

Marcus composed himself. 'Annabel, there's a reason I don't invite you to the house.'

★　★　★

198

'You're married, aren't you?' Her voice rose several octaves. Her concern from earlier had been swept away, but it had to be something big.

'No, no!' He waved his hands. 'It's nothing like that. At least, I'm not married now. I was briefly, yes.'

Marcus reached for her, but she pulled her hand away and wrapped her arms around her waist. 'So, why won't you let me come over to your place?'

'It's because of . . . Emily.'

'Emily, who is Emily?' Confusion rained down on her. 'Is this your ex-wife? Does she own the house?'

'No, no, Emily isn't my ex. Emily is, er — ' The words caught in Marcus's throat. 'Was my daughter.'

Annabel's heart sank. So, he had an ex and a daughter. This was his way of ending it; she understood now. Why had she let him into her life, into her heart? 'You know you didn't need to take me out to end it, Marcus.'

The tears she had been holding back began to slowly fall onto her cheeks.

Marcus had done it to her again, but for the last time. Annabel stood up. There was no point in staying around. Taking some notes out of her purse, she paid her share of the bill. 'Bye, Marcus.'

With one last glance, she turned and walked away. Stepping outside, she was hit by the cool sea breeze and the sound of the waves crashing against the shore. Her cheeks stung from the wind and her own salty tears that continued to fall softly down her face. Annabel wanted to look back at the restaurant but just carried on walking. She had no idea why Marcus had brought her out. He had even bought her roses! Was that so he could split up with her in a nicer way? It wasn't fair. At least her kids at the hospital would never hurt her like he just had.

She should have known he would never change. Annabel had so wanted to have a second chance with the playboy. Now all her hopes and dreams had been for nothing. She felt sick and wanted the pain in her heart to go away

— to never feel like this again for any man, love hurt too much.

She sat on a bench, the wind blowing around her. She felt lonely and totally useless. How could she ever compete? Marcus had what she so desperately wanted — a loving home, a spouse, and a child of her own. Annabel knew she was an idiot for thinking someone like him could ever love her. But she loved him so desperately. He had become her best friend, her lover, and so much more, but that was over now.

'Sweets, you need to listen. Please, hear me out.'

Annabel jumped at the sound of footsteps behind her, too caught up in her own grief to bother with what anyone else was doing.

'Marcus, leave me alone.'

'No, not till you know everything, and then if you want to walk away, you can, and I won't try to stop you.' He sat beside her, turning Annabel's face until she looked at him. Marcus gently brushed a tear away with his finger. 'Please don't cry, sweets.'

★ ★ ★

Okay, here goes nothing. He just had to wait for the fallout he was positive would come. He would tell Annabel the truth, even if it cost him everything. Before she walked into his life again, he had felt empty and alone. Annabel had given him a sense of purpose; she made him feel more alive than he ever had in the past few years.

'I was married. Everything seemed okay until Josie became pregnant. Then she changed totally when Emily was born.'

'I don't — '

Marcus placed his finger on her lips to quieten her, desperate to keep talking, to get it all out, and tell her the truth of his soul. He knew that when he finished talking, it would be up to her whether she walked out of his life forever, so he pushed on, desperate to bind her to him. 'One day, I came home from work and Josie had gone. A note said Emily was with a neighbor, and Josie wasn't coming back.'

'But . . . '

Marcus kept talking ignoring her protests that she didn't need or want to hear any of this.

'I received divorce papers pretty quickly after she had left. Then again, Josie was never one to wait for anything. She gave me full custody of Emily and declared that she didn't want to see her daughter again.'

Marcus watched her intently; his unshed tears blurred his vision.

'How can anyone not want to see their child?'

'Emily was five when she became ill with meningitis, but the doctors couldn't save her.' His voice cracked. 'The doctors at Oakwood hospital couldn't save her.'

'I try to keep all my kids safe, we all do. I never want them to die; sometimes, no matter how hard we try, we can't save them.'

'I didn't mean . . . ' Marcus pulled her toward him, wrapping her up in his arms. 'Anna, don't cry, please. I don't go to the house much because all Emily's things lie just where she left them.'

Annabel had been such a fool — he was still grieving for his daughter.

'Does Josie know about her daughter?'

'No, I never told her; I'm not even sure where she is.'

Annabel felt even worse than she had earlier. Her hand instinctively held her stomach. How could he have faced all this alone? 'Marcus, you need to find Josie and tell her. She has a right to know that her daughter has . . . ' Even she couldn't say the words.

Annabel suddenly felt very sick. It must have been that prawn pâté. 'Is that why I have never been to your house?'

'Every time I open the door, I hear Emily's laughter just for a minute, but then I remember she is no longer there.'

Silent tears fell down Marcus's face. 'I don't want to face the emptiness, so I don't go there unless I have to. I wouldn't take you to a place so full of sadness.' Marcus turned from her and looked out toward the sea. 'Emily would light up any room she entered. She was so small and tiny for her age.' The words obviously caught in his throat. 'You would have loved her. She loved to color and look at the old photographs I have. We could spend hours as I told her where they were all taken and who was in them.'

He felt Annabel's arm over his shoulders. Marcus wasn't sure what Annabel would do; he didn't know what to do. *Come on, you're thirty-seven years old and should know what you're doing.*

★   ★   ★

Annabel took a deep breath. She had to stand firm. There was no way she could cave in now. She had to let Marcus go

205

no matter how hard it was going to be. Unfortunately, it might not be the right thing to do. 'Marcus, listen. Go and find Josie. Tell her about Emily. Maybe you can rekindle what you two had in the beginning,' she said sadly. 'Only you can decide what you want to do. I just know I can't do this anymore.' Anabel didn't want to lose Marcus, but she also couldn't stand in the way of two parents' grief. Marcus was living his every day. Emily's mum still had to discover the loss of her daughter, and that made her angry.

'Do what?' A look of confusion crossed Marcus's face, but she wouldn't let it deter her.

'I knew you were hiding something, but you cannot be so callous and not tell your ex-wife about Emily.' Annabel stood. 'No matter how much you have come to dislike her, she has a right to know.'

'No, she doesn't have any rights at all.'

Annabel leaned over and kissed

Marcus on the cheek. 'Goodbye,' she whispered.

She needed to get home. Her head was beginning to spin. She couldn't fall ill, not when so many people were relying on her at work. Did food poisoning work so quickly? Doctors were always the worst at diagnosing themselves. She had often over-thought things before. At least this time, she had walked away from Marcus and not the other way around.

It took her nearly an hour to walk home. Annabel hadn't any tears left. Maybe a holiday would do her good. After all the upheaval over the past few weeks, no one could blame her for needing some me-time.

One thing she was grateful for was Marcus didn't know how much she loved him, how much she would always love him. Annabel couldn't remember even telling him that she did love him — had she? Oh, she could second-guess herself all she wanted to, but it wouldn't do anyone any good, not now.

At least, she had been spared that humiliation. She had made a fool of herself with Marcus for the last time.

Annabel looked at her watch — nine o'clock. She needed Rachel to come round and tell her everything would be okay. She was in uncharted waters. She'd had casual dates but nothing serious. All her girlfriends thought she was daft with her plan to stay away from men for career advancement. Most of her friends had married or had long-term partners whilst she went to the same parties or functions alone.

★　★　★

Marcus sat on the bench looking into the space that had been Annabel a few moments ago. He thought of going after her. But what would be the point? She wasn't bothered. Annabel was right about one thing, though. He would have to tell Josie about Emily. He didn't want his ex-wife turning up and wondering where her daughter was.

Marcus didn't know where to start. He'd have to hire a detective to find her. Then it would be another conversation he didn't want to have.

Marcus drove around all night. He hadn't wanted to go back to the hotel and couldn't go to the house. Seeing Annabel was totally out of the question. He felt useless and lost again. He needed Annabel. She had given him his spirit back, filled the empty space in his heart — the part that was just for him. No one else could have done that.

First things first. He would sort out the Josie problem, and then he would see if he could win Annabel back. Marcus was determined not to give up on his happiness. He could live again, be the person he wanted to be, not just the guy in a suit crunching numbers. He had made himself extremely rich doing so, but no amount of money would bring him the happiness he craved. Only Annabel could do that, and this time she was not going to get away from him.

Marcus drove up to the house, shaking his head as he got out of the car. The garden was so overgrown; it was bringing down the entire neighborhood. He would have to sort that out as well. How could he not have seen this before? *So you're going to see all this when you can't be bothered to even come to your own house?* Taking a huge breath, he opened the door. It was time to sort his life out. Tatty Christmas decorations still adorned most of the pictures and hung from the walls. The Christmas tree sat unloved in the corner of the living room; presents for them both sat huddled underneath. He looked closely at the piles of new toys. Attached to the base of the Christmas tree lay an envelope. Written in pink crayon were the words 'To Santa.' He took it off the tree and placed it in his suit pocket. It was unusual for Emily to write a letter to Santa to get Christmas Eve.

Wishing he could turn back time wasn't going to do any good. Marcus picked up one of Emily's little doll dresses and held it lovingly in his hands. 'I'm sorry, my darling. I need to put your toys away,' he said, choking back a sob. It was time to lay his ghosts to rest and move on. To what, he didn't know.

Annabel had surprised him. She had been so callous, or she had all the appearance of it. After he had thought about it, he knew why she had done what she had. That was the old Annabel, never one to be pushy. She would make the decision, and if she felt it was best for everyone to walk away, so be it.

Marcus hoped that Emily would understand. He would just keep them in her room until he had the courage to give them to another little girl so she could have as much enjoyment out of them as his own beautiful girl had. Wandering into the kitchen, he grabbed a few boxes out of the larder. Then walking around the house, he put all Emily's toys in the boxes.

Tears streamed down his face. 'You're stronger than this, Marcus.' He had never done anything this hard before. Marcus wished Annabel was there with him. She always said the right thing. Annabel seemed to be able to see right into his soul and know exactly what he was thinking. The stairs creaked as he walked slowly to the second floor, the noise echoing around the empty house.

'I used to love hearing you laugh. Do you remember playing hide and seek when it rained?' As he reached the last stair, he paused. Maybe he should just make a keepsake box and have a few of her things in it, 'I bet you would have liked a time capsule.' Marcus knew what people would say if they heard him talking to himself, but it was bringing Emily closer to him.

Emily's name plaque stared at him. His breath felt like stones in his lungs. His ribs still hurt, but it was his heart giving him the most pain. Marcus opened the door slowly. It, like everything else in this place, was falling apart through lack of use and the love these walls used to share. Now it was a hollow shell, a shadow of what had once been, just like he was.

Putting the boxes down on the bed, he took one last look around his daughter's room, then sat on her bed, and took out the letter to Santa Claus. He opened it carefully. 'Your writing has got neater.'

Dear Santa, could I please have this, love Emily. It was a picture of a family and a house.

'Oh, Emily.' She had drawn him and her with a mum and a little sister as well. So that is what she wanted, a family, and she was asking Santa to give it to her.

'You would have loved my Anna,' he whispered as he placed the picture back in his pocket. Perhaps he could show Annabel. Then he remembered that she had just walked away from him. 'I know I should have told her about you. But I was scared that Annabel wouldn't understand,' Marcus said out loud. 'Emily, what can I do?'

But Emily would not answer him, she couldn't. *Stop being ridiculous, Marcus.* He liked talking to her, sometimes. It kept her alive for him. He never wanted to let go, to move on. It would mean forgetting. How could he forget the child he had looked after, loved for five years, only to have her snatched away from him?

His heart seemed to get lighter, and a strange sort of peace descended on him while he sat on her bed. He couldn't understand what was going on. Marcus was usually so keyed up about work at home, and now nothing seemed to matter. There was no point stressing about things he couldn't change, to worry about how he could relive the past. All that seemed to matter now was a future.

'I'm going to set up the Emily Chapman Foundation. To help sick children live their dreams.' The idea had sprung from the darkest depths of his mind. He could use this house for it. Let parents with seriously ill children stay here while they visited their children.

Taking out his phone, he typed a text to Mary telling her of his idea. She would sort everything out. He couldn't live in this house again, but neither could he sell it and lose Emily. She was here in this house, in the furniture. Her voice echoed off the walls and into his heart.

Leaving Emily's room wasn't as hard as he thought it would be, not this time. His little girl would always be with him — in this house, in his heart, his mind, until he joined her wherever she was.

Marcus walked into the spare room where he had put Josie's things she had left behind. Pictures and knick-knacks, things he was going to give Emily when she had got a bit older. He knew where to find the photo of his ex-wife, buried under a mountain of clothes.

Taking out his mobile, he made a quick call to his friend at the office. 'Hi, it's Marcus. I need you to hire a private investigator to find Josie. I will text you a photo.'

Now for that spare room. He had no need for Josie's things, not anymore. He ambled downstairs for the black bags. Taking them up to the room, he systematically put everything that had once belonged to Josie in them, throwing all the bags over the landing to the floor below. The bin men weren't going to be happy.

Just when he had given up any hope of receiving a phone call today, his phone rang. 'Hello . . . She works where? . . . Right, okay, thanks.' That was quick.

Marcus knew that not telling Josie before now had cost him a second chance at happiness with Annabel. Josie would not interfere with his life again, not after this. He regretted even getting involved with her in the first place. He headed to the kitchen and decided to sort out all the cupboards, slamming each drawer and cupboard door shut.

Emily was gone, and he couldn't bring her back. He knew that, but he also knew that his little princess wouldn't have minded having a sister. Not if the picture was anything to go by.

Clearing the bin bags from the hall, he grabbed his car keys and set off to see Josie. A necessary evil as his mother would say. It took him nearly three hours to get to Birmingham. The traffic was horrendous; Marcus had no idea what reception he would get. Not a good one, that was for sure.

Entering Josie's office building, Marcus took a quick look around. Sleek lines and lots of light, an architect's dream. 'I'm here to see Josie Chapman.'

The receptionist eyed him suspiciously. 'And you are?'

'Her ex-husband.' It actually felt good saying that.

'I will just call up and see if she will see you.' The receptionist quickly made a call. 'She will be down in a moment.'

Marcus wandered over to the leather sofas and sat down. Josie always kept him waiting. The hands on the clock ticked slowly by. This was going to be one of the worst things he had done. Why had Annabel insisted he do this? Ever since she had come back into his life, he felt like he had been hit by a truck.

'What do you want, Marcus?' Josie stood before him, her brown hair cut into a neat bob and a black trouser suit made her look ever the business woman he remembered.

'We need to talk. It's about Emily.'

'How many times do I have to tell you? Emily is your problem. I don't want anything to do with her.' Josie turned to leave. 'I gave her to you as having a child seemed so important to the ever high-and-mighty Marcus Chapman. I don't want involved in any problems you may or may not have.'

'I am not high and mighty, thank you.' Marcus's ire had risen. Now how should he tell her, gently or bluntly?

'Emily's dead.' A harsh statement and not how he had planned to break the news. He knew how he sounded, but as she didn't care, he wasn't going to care about how he told her.

It had the desired effect. 'What . . . what happened to her?'

Marcus looked at Josie. Her bottom lip was quivering. 'She had meningitis, but it was too late to do anything.' Marcus's whole body shook as a mix of anger and pain whirled around inside him.

'I didn't know. I'm sorry for you, but she wasn't my child.' Josie looked stony-faced. The brief look of guilty sadness was quickly replaced with Josie's usual demeanor.

Didn't that selfish bitch have a heart? Emily was just as much her daughter as his, and now she was gone. What the hell was that all about?

'Fine. I thought you should know.' Walking a little distance away, he added, 'I see I have just wasted my time.'

He didn't wait for a reply. He preferred to walk out of the building rather than tell her what he really thought. Did Annabel seriously think that he and Josie would get back together? Honestly, that woman drove him crazy. Hadn't he shown Anna just what she had meant to him, what she had always meant to him?

Marcus's heart sank. He had lost everything, first Emily and now Annabel. Was there any way he could win her back?

11

Marcus stood outside Josie's office building casting one last sad glance, a final goodbye to that part of his life. He wasn't sad about Josie, just her heartlessness and the loss of a daughter who he would never see grow from a happy young girl to a terrible teenager, or get to walk up the aisle on her wedding day. There was no getting away from the history he and Josie had shared, but it was a history that could now thankfully be buried forever in the darkest part of his brain. Whilst Emily — his precious little girl — the only person who had loved him unconditionally, would remain forever in his heart.

Marcus still hadn't told Annabel what he had discovered with the accounts. There hadn't seemed to be enough time before she walked away.

How the hell that woman had come up with the idiotic idea that, because of Emily, he would repair his relationship with Josie and say goodbye to what could have been a future with her boggled his mind. Women sometimes!

Taking his phone out of his back pocket, he dialed Mr. Underwood's number. 'Could I speak to Mr. Underwood please?'

'Yes, just one moment.' The voice on the other end seemed smooth and cold.

Within a few minutes, Marcus had the chairman of the board on the line. 'Mr. Underwood, I wonder if I could set up a business meeting with you today.' He waited for an answer. 'It would need to be in private. I wouldn't want certain people overhearing. Perhaps we could meet this evening over at the Grand Hotel? They have a very nice bistro restaurant.'

Receiving the confirmation he needed, Marcus arranged for the meeting to take place at seven that evening. One thing that had surprised him was that the chairman hadn't been surprised to hear from someone, almost as though he knew what Marcus had wanted without it being spoken of.

On the way back, Marcus's mind overflowed with Annabel. She had accessed the files without permission, even though she had been given the details. 'Could she get arrested for hacking?' he mumbled to himself. Who had sent her the information and why? Perhaps, if he could unravel everything and solve the mystery, Annabel might want him back. At the beginning, he had thought it was just a bit of fun, giving something back. Marcus had no idea how over the space of a few days he could fall so heavily in love with Annabel all over again. He had been hit by a steamroller, and for once, he had no idea whether he was coming, going, or even left the building.

His dreams swirled with memories of them lying together, of playing childish games on the beach. He felt emptier now than he ever had before. He had hated himself for keeping things from her, but once he had admitted them, he couldn't take them back. Would Annabel have preferred to remain in blissful ignorance of everything in his life?

Marcus had been around the block more than once. Meaningless one-night stands satisfied his urges but left him feeling as empty and unhappy as before. One night with Annabel had meant everything. He never usually went in for feelings like this. Marcus preferred to keep a distance from everyone and his morbid sense of self-preservation to himself. Annabel had broken down his resolve the minute he saw her again. The only thing for certain was that the happiness he felt could only be found in Annabel's loving arms. By the time he had fought through the traffic jams and got back to Brighton, it was nearly time for his meeting. His ribs had started to hurt again from doing too much in one day.

'Would you like me to park your car,

sir?' the valet asked him.

'Sure, I won't need it till tomorrow,' he replied quickly, grabbing the envelope out of the glove box and handing the valet his car keys.

Marcus wandered slowly into the hotel and into the Bistro. Soft lighting lit up the white linen tablecloths as soft jazz played in the background. He'd had the foresight to book a table for him and a guest. But he had no idea who that guest looked like apart from his name.

A rather dapper gentleman with a black walking stick and top hat walked into the restaurant. He seemed more suitable to the Victorian era than the twenty-first century, but he supposed this was an era where anything went fashion wise.

The waiter approached with the strange gentleman in tow. 'Your guest has arrived, sir. Mr. Underwood.'

Marcus stood and shook the man's hand. 'Very pleased to meet you.' He hated being so formal, but he wasn't someone he knew and it was only right.

'Oh, Thomas, please. I don't usually go in for the formalities myself.'

'Marcus. Would you like to order first?'

'No, you called this meeting, and I must say I am intrigued.' Mr. Underwood's voice sounded rather scratchy and rough.

'One of your doctors, Annabel Simpson, received a very strange phone call and then an email.' Marcus paused to judge his companion's reaction, but there wasn't one. The man kept his face a mask. 'In the email were log-in details for the hospital accounts.'

'Ahh, so she did receive the email. I did wonder,' replied Mr. Underwood.

'You sent the email and gave the phone call?' Marcus tried to hide his surprise.

'Yes, she phoned me just after her meeting with Mr. Wild about the children's ward. I must say I was quite surprised with what she had to say.'

'Did you think it strange then?'

'Most definitely strange. There was always enough money for the hospital to run efficiently and to full capacity without closures. Yet over the last three years, there have been threats of closures of several wards.'

Marcus tried to keep up as Mr. Underwood sped up his speech. 'I knew something wasn't quite right. All I get each year is a fiscal report, and the figures seem to add up, but the hospital is struggling for money.'

'I'm an accountant, and I have looked into the figures which Annabel . . . ' Marcus corrected himself. 'Er . . . Doctor Simpson gave me. There are, I believe, two people involved, although I cannot be sure about that. You need to contact the police.' Marcus took the printed pages out of the envelope and handed them to his guest. 'If you see where I have highlighted, that is where the money is going. Fortunately, whoever has been doing it hasn't done a good job.'

'They fooled me,' Mr. Underwood

replied, his eyes downcast.

'I knew when Anna told me what Mrs. Higginbottom told her — you use a third-party company to buy equipment — that was where the money was going. From there, goodness knows where it has gone.' Marcus felt sorry for the chairman, who would possibly lose his position for this. Someone knew what they were doing and covering up enough so it wouldn't be easily be spotted unless you knew where to look and for what.

The elder gentleman shook his head. 'We don't use a third-party to buy equipment. The hospital buys it themselves. As and when it is needed.' What had been going on finally dawned on Mr. Underwood. The poor man looked green.

'You need to get the police involved and get whoever is the one doing the accounts questioned.' Handing over the rest of the paperwork to Mr. Underwood, he said, 'Here. I think you'll need these. There's just one thing?'

'Just name it.'

'Annabel shouldn't have accessed the information. I don't want her in any trouble. The police can question me if they so wish, but Dr. Simpson has to stay out of trouble.'

'Don't worry. As I was the one who phoned her and gave her the passwords, I guarantee you there will be no trouble.' His guest took a sip of his wine 'The day Annabel phoned me, I was concerned. Yes, every hospital has cuts, maybe the new high-tech equipment you want would have to wait for another year, but the cuts wouldn't be enough to shut a ward down.'

'Mr. Wild has tried shutting down the ward before. Why the same one?' inquired Marcus.

'I don't know the answer to that, unless because it is a high-dependency ward. The money for its upkeep is larger than for say a basic ward.'

Marcus thought about everything. 'And that would mean more money could be stolen if it wasn't going to the kids.'

'Exactly, it seems such a simple plan now that we are discussing it like this. I will be forever in your debt, young man.' Mr. Underwood shook Marcus's hand. 'Please don't worry about Doctor Simpson. She is one of our best assets.'

Marcus nodded but said no more. Everything that needed to be said had been. The two men shook hands again and parted company. Marcus had done all he could do, and all that was left for him was to sit back, wait, and watch. He took out his phone and started to text Anna. No, she didn't want anything to do with him. *Why did you walk away?* Marcus was determined to win her back, but he had no idea how on earth he would do that. To hell with it. He penned a simple text message — *can I see you?* She would no doubt ignore it, but at least Annabel would know he was thinking about her until he could formulate a plan.

As he took the lift up to his hotel

room, his phone started ringing. Annabel. Just as he was about to answer it went dead. Had she meant to phone him, or was it an accident and she meant to phone someone else? When she didn't ring again, the only thing he could conclude was she had rung him by accident.

★　★　★

Annabel canceled the call and put her phone down, which was stupid. What if he had picked it up? She had only wanted to listen to his voice on the answering machine. But she had forgotten to hide her number. Hopefully, Marcus would think she had called by accident, and she prayed he wouldn't phone her back. She missed him more than she thought she ever would.

Her phone flashed and beeped indicating a message, and she picked the device up cautiously as though it would burn her. Annabel's heart skipped a beat as she read Marcus's message. No, she wouldn't see him. She couldn't, the pain of being told he was with Josie would be too much to bear. Now that was a question. Could you actually be jealous of someone you didn't know?

Rachel — that's who she needed, and a girly night with her best friend. Would she come, though?

Annabel dialed Rachel's number. It rang for what seemed like an eternity before it was answered. 'Rach, any chance you can come round?'

'Half an hour, babe. I'm just having dinner,' Rachel replied.

★   ★   ★

'I really hope you know what you're doing, Rachel.'

Rachel looked lovingly at Dr. Walker. 'Don't worry, darling, I do. Annabel and Marcus need to sort themselves out.'

Rachel looked around the hotel bar; it had a very upmarket feel to it, leather seating, and soft lights. She had done her research into Mr. Chapman and found out all about his past seeing as Annabel had been extremely vague on the whole subject. She could tell when they had first met on the ride, there was an undercurrent of sexual tension between them. Something had happened, and all that business at the service station. Suddenly, out of the corner of her eye, she spotted Marcus sitting alone at a comer table.

Wandering over, Rachel took a deep breath. 'Marcus?'

Marcus looked up at her nonchalantly. 'Yes?' His voice was flat and lifeless.

'I don't know if you remember me.' She shifted from foot to foot. 'I'm Rachel, Annabel's friend.'

'Is something wrong with Anna?'

'No, no, not at all,' Rachel replied, waving her hands in front of her. 'It's just that she's been so sad, and I thought that maybe . . . '

'What? Maybe it had something to

do with me?' Marcus took a long slow sip of his drink. 'She was the one that ended things.'

'Maybe she had a reason for it, or maybe she just didn't want to get in the way.'

'Of what? I'm not doing anything.' Marcus stood up, 'I don't mean to be rude, Rachel, but I've nothing more to say.'

Rachel watched Marcus wander away. Well, that went well, didn't it, she thought to herself. Any fool could see he loved her friend, and if Annabel would only admit it to herself, she was in love with him. What was keeping them apart?

'Darling, don't you have to go and see Annabel?'

'Yes, and perhaps I could persuade her to tell me everything.' Rachel reached up and kissed her boyfriend. 'I knew there was a good reason I was with you, Dr. Walker.'

★ ★ ★

Annabel slouched back in her armchair; at least for a while tonight, she wouldn't be alone. Her heart ached, and she felt like a large part of her was missing. Marcus was missing; she missed his goofy laugh, those sexy black biker leathers of his. The way her name rolled off his tongue, his strong muscular arms wrapped around her. She loved him, loved him in a way she hadn't loved any other man. A feeling of bereavement washed over her. He would never be hers.

Marcus had a right to start again with Josie, and she wasn't going to stand in his way. The two of them deserved to be happy. At least this time, she had a happy memory of them being together. She couldn't blame him. She had walked away, knowing that if she didn't at least give him a chance to be with Josie, she would never forgive herself.

She thought back to when she first moved to the house 8 months ago. Marcus hadn't even been in her thoughts, nothing had except to start again. That feeling of needing to belong had been really strong. But her two bedroom house with a sea view was turning into one big nightmare. She barely knew any of the neighbors, her only real friend was Rachel, and she had her own life to lead. Looking around her kitchen, packing boxes and black bin liners still sat around the room. Loads of stuff that had been bought as an *I'll use it once I'm settled in* item but had never bothered.

The worst thing about living in Brighton as opposed to Sompting or any other small town in Sussex was she didn't know that many people. At least in Sompting, she had grown up with her friends, but as was so often the case, people had moved away, creating lives for themselves, and she had moved to Brighton for her job. She was too busy at work to form close bonds with anyone. The next-door neighbor had done some shopping for her when she couldn't because she had worked two days straight.

Opening the front door every day, she was greeted with an empty silence. She would sometimes shout hello, to make herself feel better. It made Annabel sad not to have anyone to discuss her day or to go out with for meals. Rachel didn't need her constant whining and moaning about things just because she was feeling lonely and sad.

Annabel wondered if she should get a parrot. At least that way, she would have someone to talk to at night and sit on the sofa with her to watch television.

Annabel opened the heavy oak door. 'Hey, Rach.'

'Hey, honey.' Rachel greeted her friend in her usual cheerful manner.

Annabel just stood, one hand on the front door.

'Are you going to invite me in? Or am I going to stand outside all night?'

'Sorry, I'm not with it. Come through to the kitchen.' Annabel moved to the side and allowed her friend into the house.

'You going somewhere?'

Her friend looked at all her unpacked bags and boxes. 'No, I decided to get the boxes out and finally sort them out. I'd thrown them all in the garage but thought maybe it was time to make this more of a home.' Picking a small bag up, she tossed it toward the stairs. 'I'm going to put it all in the spare room when I have the energy.'

'Oh, come on. I thought you liked it here?'

'I do. It's just that . . . ' The words caught in Annabel's throat. 'Do you know how many people I talk to at home excluding you and the neighbor?'

'Go on, then. Surprise me.'

'None, Rach. I sit here alone every night with the stupid television to keep me company.'

'Come on. Let's get this bottle open,' Rachel replied, waving the bottle around.

'But you never know. I might get

sacked before that.'

'You're not going to get sacked, Annabel.' Rachel held the bottle aloft. 'You know, I'm not sure this is a good idea.'

'No, I think we need to chill out.' It would be a miracle if she could relax. Annabel's mind always turned over like a bullet train. 'You get the corkscrew, and I will find us some glasses.' She pointed toward the kitchen drawer as she rattled around in the cupboard looking for two wine glasses.

'You know, hun, Mr. Wild was totally wrong for threatening you. I mean, who the hell does he think he is?'

'How on earth did you know about that?' she said, placing the glasses on the counter.

'You know Mr. Wild, always one to talk about someone behind their back.'

Seeing her friend shrug her shoulders didn't make her feel any better. Is that how it was? The slime ball would say jump, and everyone would meekly reply how high. Annabel herself had been guilty of that, but not anymore. She wasn't going to be a pushover.

Rachel was always sympathetic toward her plight. She gripped the kitchen counter. It made her so angry that Mr. Wild wouldn't listen to anyone. God, that man was a law unto himself.

'Annabel, let's go sit down so we can have a proper chat.'

Annabel just nodded and wandered into the living room.

Photographs of the Sussex Downs adorned the walls and several Regency pieces had pride of place on the furniture. Her prized possession was her tea caddy from 1815 that unusually still had its key. If that little box could only talk and tell her of all the ladies it had served.

She watched Rachel looking round her eclectic living room. 'You know, your obsession with Mr. Darcy is taking over.'

Annabel put on her best Mrs. Bennet voice. 'You're just jealous that you don't have a tea caddy.'

She felt a little better with the teasing. A glass of wine and good company were just what the doctor ordered. As long as memories of biker Marcus Chapman didn't interrupt. Closing her eyes briefly, she could see his face. His eyes, the way he had looked angrily at her. Yet there was something hidden in his jeweled eyes, a spark trying to break free of the chains he had created.

'Earth to Annabel.'

Annabel quickly opened her eyes; a flush of heat hit her face. 'Sorry, honey. I was just thinking.'

Holding the bottle over Annabel's glass, Rach topped it up. 'What about?'

'Marcus.'

'Okay, what has got you so wired?'

'I should never have let him go. I should have held on,' Annabel replied sadly. 'I mean, he has suffered a huge loss, one that we are confronted with every day, and what do I? I hightail it out of there.'

Rachel stood up. 'You got any ice cream?'

'Yes, in the freezer. The bowls are in the cupboard above the microwave.'

Her friend returned quickly with two bowls of the sweet, creamy dessert. 'Here, it will make you feel better.'

'Mmm.' But Annabel didn't believe in the almighty power of ice cream.

'Look, you have to see it from Marcus's point of view. He seems like someone used to sorting things out for himself, not relying on anyone else. He's not one to be taken care of.' Rachel took a spoonful of ice cream but continued, 'You two obviously have some history, which, by the way, you still haven't told me all of.'

Annabel hadn't thought of that. She had been just the same, wanting to do everything to help the people on the ward that were suffering. But she couldn't and had to leave it to the nurses on duty to share in the work. 'Well, he isn't going to want anything to do with me now, is he? I told him when we were by the sea front to go to his ex-wife, and I haven't talked to him since he called me. At least I never fell in love with him.'

The little voice in Annabel's head goaded her. *You've just lied to your best friend. You love him more than anything.*

'That's the spirit,' Rachel replied, holding up her spoon.

Annabel copied her, and the spoons made a tinkling noise when they met each other.

'Look, if he wants to just give up on your relationship, then I don't see why you don't just move on. Find somebody who truly cares about you.'

Annabel knew Rachel was being nice, but she didn't understand the whole situation. Her life had been best when Marcus had been there. The way he had looked at her so tenderly when they made love. People who just want one thing don't do that, do they? She wasn't alone; she had felt cared for and loved. The last thing she needed was for

Rachel to do the bitchy girl thing on her. Yes, that was okay for those relationships with complete Neanderthals but not her Marcus.

'I just can't, Rachel. I can't forget him.' Annabel couldn't stop from pondering a future, one that no longer had Marcus in it. She didn't want to think about it.

After a brief silence, the conversation changed to other topics, and Marcus was left behind. Rachel didn't stay late. When she had gone, Annabel wandered out into the garden. The house felt like it was closing in on her. She needed an escape — anything to take her mind of Marcus. His looks, his voice made her forget herself. She had no idea what was going on in her own mind.

Annabel stared out into the darkness hoping to find an answer to her problems.

12

'Hey, Annabel, you don't look so great,' Rachel said as they did the rounds of the children's ward together.

'I've not felt great since I went to Leon's restaurant. I guess I must have picked up a bug or something.' Annabel looked down at the floor. Her belly had bulged out a bit. 'I think I need to go on a diet as well. I seem to have put on a bit of weight since Marcus and I split.'

'You've not heard from him?'

Rachel run her hand down her arm. 'No, but then I don't expect to.' She looked at her chart. 'Come on, last patient of the day. Let's give Tracy the good news.'

Tracy was one of their heart patients, and today was the day she could go home. Annabel didn't ever want Tracy to come back because it would mean her heart surgery had failed.

'Changing the subject, are you?' replied Rachel. 'Okay, come on then.'

'Come on then, what?'

'If you don't want me talking about Marcus, what shall we talk about?'

'We don't have to talk about anything,' snapped Annabel.

'You have to admit that Marcus is one hot guy. I'd like him to check out under my hood.'

Annabel was getting angrier by the second; she clenched her hands tight, thrusting them to her sides. 'Listen, he isn't going to go anywhere near your hood or mine for that matter.'

She caught the sly grin on Rachel's face. 'Don't even think it. Have you got a second job?'

'What do you mean a second job?'

'As Marcus's P.A, you're doing a good job of trying to get me to change my mind about him.'

'No, I just think everyone deserves a second chance.'

'Rachel, I will not give a second

chance to that playboy. No matter how he looks.'

Annabel walked next to Rachel as an eerie silence descended over them. Had he employed her as his spin-doctor? Besides, if Annabel hadn't seen him, how on earth could Rachel know so much, or was she just good at paying attention?

'I'm sorry if I touched a nerve. I just want you to be happy, Anna.'

Annabel stopped walking. 'I know you mean well, but can you mean well with a different guy? Not one that is a two-faced so-and-so like him.'

Rachel smiled weakly. 'Perhaps.'

They had reached the corridor where the private rooms were. Stopping outside room 102, she tapped gently on the door and entered the room. Tracy sat coloring whilst her parents sat to either side of her. 'Tracy, how are you feeling?'

'Bored of sitting here.' The little girl looked up briefly before continuing her coloring.

'Well, you won't have to be bored anymore; you can go home today.' Annabel saw how Tracy's eyes light up, and the thought of letting this particular child go filled her with joy. Tracy still had a long way to go, but at least now she could enjoy her life, play with her friends at the park, and everything else a child should do. Annabel's smile filled her face.

'Thank you, thank you,' Tracy's parents exclaimed.

Annabel was having a hard time deciding who was more excited, Tracy or her parents.

'She will have to take it easy, no climbing trees or playing football for a while.' Annabel paused. 'I don't want to see you back here, Tracy. Please do what I ask.'

'I will. I promise.'

The little girl hopped off her bed and flung her arms around Annabel, sobbing.

'Don't cry, little one.'

'I'm just happy, but I'm going to miss

you, Doctor Simpson.'

'I will miss you too.' Annabel hugged her back and then handed the discharge papers to her parents. 'I will get the paperwork sorted, and then you can leave whenever you're ready.'

It was times like this that Annabel wanted a child of her own. Time was passing her by, and with no husband or boyfriend on the scene, her dream was unlikely to be realized.

As they left the room, Rachel commented, 'She won't hang around for long.'

'No, she won't. It will be great to see her leaving.' Annabel was always sad when patients went home, but happy too that she had been able to help.

'Hey, Annabel, why don't you just call him?'

'No, it's over. I'm not going to be made a fool of again.'

'What did Marcus do that was so terrible?' Rachel looked at her, and her face was flushed with anger. 'You two need your heads banged together.'

'Why's that?'

'I saw how you two were together when we went out on our double date.'

'That's ancient history.'

'Well, Anna, I don't think so. Remind me why you are apart again?'

'Just drop it, Rachel.'

'Okay, okay. How about coming out with me later?' Rachel asked.

'Aren't you seeing Dr. Walker tonight?' Annabel asked as she opened her office door.

'Yes, but I thought we could have some girly time first. We haven't done that in a long while.'

'I guess so,' Annabel conceded. 'I have some paperwork to finish.'

When Rachel had gone, Annabel wandered over to the window, opening it just a little so she could get some fresh air. The nausea hadn't gone away. No matter what tablets she had prescribed herself, she still felt just as sick. Annabel couldn't remember the last time she had eaten anything and kept it down. She hated to admit it, but maybe she should go see a doctor, because she hadn't managed to cure herself. 'You're losing your touch, Annabel,' she said to herself.

Picking up the phone, she dialed Doctor Walker's line. 'Can you see me for a few minutes?' She waited for an answer.

'I'm a bit busy, Annabel,' came Dr. Walker's blunt reply.

'Please, I don't know who else to turn too.'

Was that the cogs turning over in his head?

'Sure, but you will need to come now. I have another patient in fifteen minutes.'

'Okay, I will be right down.'

Annabel wandered down the halls. She had become extremely unsteady on her feet. It was too hot, and the sickness seemed to be getting worse. The smell of canteen food wasn't helping matters.

She knocked on Doctor Walker's door and waited for him to invite her in.

'There you are, Annabel. I wondered how long you would take.' Doctor Walker was always one for cracking jokes. 'So tell me what is wrong?'

'I just feel sick all the time. I'm barely eating, and my stomach seems to have become bloated.' Annabel carried on, 'It's ever since I had prawn pâté at a restaurant, and now I'm like this.'

'Have you prescribed yourself anything?' he asked whilst writing notes on a pad.

'Of course I have. What do you take me for?' Annabel was getting mad. What on earth was Dr. Walker thinking?

'Look, I think I know what your problem is. Just get on the couch, and undo your trousers a little.'

Annabel did as requested. As soon as she lay down, the sickness increased, and the ceiling started to spin. Doctor Walker placed his hands on her stomach and began pushing down on either side.

'What are you doing?'
'Annabel, you're not ill.'

'So why do I feel like this?'

'Because I think you're pregnant. An ultrasound will tell us for sure. When was the last time you had sex?'

Normally, Annabel would be embarrassed at this sort of questioning by a total stranger, but he wasn't. *Pull yourself together girl.* 'About ten weeks ago-ish.'

'Your symptoms point to a severe case of morning sickness. You need to take some time off work. I will prescribe something that should help. Drink plenty of fluids and eat small meals. Dry toast and biscuits if you feel like you can't eat much.'

'I'm . . . I'm pregnant? How?'

Doctor Walker laughed at her. 'I'm sure you don't need me to tell you that.'

Marcus's name jumped to her lips, but she wouldn't say it out loud. She couldn't. It was his child she carried, and now she was even more confused than ever. She missed him so much.

'This may seem like a stupid

question, but do you know who the father is?'

'Yes, but he isn't going to want to know.'

'Such a shame,' replied Doctor Walker, shaking his head. 'You can get up now if you want to.'

Annabel sat up slowly; she couldn't believe she was pregnant. But she knew she was strong enough to bring up the child on her own; she would need to juggle work with being a mum. Just the thought of having someone to love of her own made her entire being fill with joy.

She and Rachel could go around shopping for baby things. The spare room could be decorated and made into a nursery. Perhaps they could have a look tomorrow, seeing as they were both off work at the same time for once.

'Thanks, Doctor Walker. How far gone am I, do you think?'

'Let me just do an ultrasound to make sure my suspicions are right.

About ten weeks, I should say. With any luck, the morning sickness should wear off soon.'

Annabel thanked him again and rushed off to find Rachel. She would have to tell her before Doctor Walker let something slip. She found her friend in the canteen having her break. 'Rach, guess what? You'll never guess,' Annabel said excitedly.

'You're pregnant,' Rachel replied in a serious tone.

'How did you know?'

'Because it's obvious. You've put on a bit of weight, and you're sick most of the time.'

Annabel didn't appreciate her friend laughing at her. 'If you knew, how come I didn't know? It's my body.'

Rachel picked up her tea and took a small sip. 'You were too caught up in your breakup with Marcus to even notice.'

'I guess you're right. Do you want to meet me in town tomorrow? We could go have a look for some nursery things?' Annabel's excitement was growing.

'Yes, of course, I will go with you. The question is, are you going to tell Marcus about the baby?'

'How . . . '

Rachel interrupted her. 'How did I know it was Marcus's baby? He's the only one you've slept with in months.'

'Okay, okay, so that's a dead giveaway.' She had wanted a child of her own, so there was no question of her not keeping the child. In a way, she hoped that her son or daughter would look like its father. She would always have Marcus with her no matter what happened in the future.

'So are you going to tell him?'

Annabel didn't think he would be interested, with no contact since that night after the restaurant other than one text. She was almost positive he was making a go of it with Josie. Maybe the loss of their child had brought them together. 'No, Rach, I'm not. He has no need to know. He wouldn't be interested in having to put up with me permanently in his life because of a child. I'm going to finish early go home and get the tablets I've been prescribed.'

'Look, tell me to butt out if you want, but he does have a right to know,' Rachel said sternly.

'He doesn't have any right. It's my baby. He's made himself clear.'

'Hang on. No, he told you about the child he lost, and you walked away. How is that his fault?'

Annabel didn't want to admit that her friend was right.

'How could he tell you something like that when you first met up again?' Rachel's voice rose. 'You two didn't even know that you would get along. He has a right to keep some things private.'

'What, even from me? That is just so wrong.' Annabel took several deep breaths. 'I don't want to argue with you. I'm going home.'

Rachel watched as her friend left. Then she stared at her cup. This wasn't right. Surely, Marcus had a right to know. He had already lost one child, and Annabel was making sure he lost another that he didn't even know about.

Taking her phone out, she Googled Marcus Chapman. Dialing the number, she kept her fingers crossed that it was the right one. 'Marcus, it's Rachel, Annabel's friend. I really need to speak to you.' She stopped for a minute. 'I will meet you at Madera Drive in half an hour.'

Rachel took a huge breath. Annabel wouldn't thank her for doing this, but there was no way she could sit back and do nothing. Picking up her bag, Rachel left the dregs of her tea and set off on her mission. There was no time to even talk to her boyfriend. People could be so stupid sometimes. She had seen Annabel and Marcus together.

Any fool could see that he loved her as much as she did him.

* * *

Marcus leaned back in his chair just as his secretary walked in.

'Anything else you need, Mr. Chapman?'

'Er . . . no, it's okay, Mrs. Windbourne.' Marcus thought for a moment. 'Do you remember Annabel?' He never called her Mary in front of other employees. He didn't want to show favoritism. He knew how some of the other employees thought already. He didn't want to make the situation worse.

'Oh, that's that pretty young thing you brought in here, isn't it.'

It was more a statement of fact than a question. 'You have any idea how I can win her back?'

'Mr. Chapman, whatever do you mean?' She closed the door and sat in the chair opposite. 'Are you really going to tell me that you let her get away?'

'I told her about Emily.' His eyes scanned his desk, anywhere but at his motherly secretary. 'She told me to find Josie and said goodbye.'

'Perhaps she thought you and Josie would get back together. I never did like the woman. Gold digger, she was. I can smell them a mile off.'

Marcus chuckled. Well, the gold digger part might have been right. Since the divorce settlement, his pocket had been lightened considerably. 'That was true, unfortunately, and she saw Emily as an inconvenience to her lavish lifestyle and trips to Saint-Tropez with all her friends.' Picking up his pen, he twirled it around in his fingers. 'She didn't seem bothered that I had lost Emily. What a selfish bitch.' He held back the tears, the pain still too raw for him. Seeing Josie again and her damn attitude toward everything made it all ten times worse. Why had Annabel decided to leave him alone, just when he was beginning to find that special love, love that had eluded him for so many years, a pure satisfying love?

'People do silly things when they are in love.'

'But Anna wasn't in love with me. She never said anything of the sort.' Marcus was totally frustrated.

'Honestly, men. You never listen to your own hearts. Always ruled by the head.' Mary brushed the creases out of her skirt. 'Why don't you go see her at the hospital?' Mary had a devious twinkle in her eye. 'That way she can't run away from you and will have to stand there and talk to you.'

He shook his head. What if she called hospital security on him, then what? His fighting spirit was leaving him well behind. No, this was one time he was going to win. Twice he had lost Annabel. The first time he had let her go; this time she was going to be his wife. 'Good idea, thank you, dear.' Marcus stood up and gave her a hug. He would never have got through all the traumas if it weren't for her.

'Annabel's friend wants to meet me in half an hour. Not sure why.'

'Look, you go, and I will lock the office for the day. Maybe after the meeting with her friend you can go and see Annabel.'

'You're the best. You know that, right?' With that said, Marcus picked up his coat and left the office. Rachel was a nice girl, but since he had split with Annabel he hadn't seen or spoken to her. So it had come as a bit of a shock for her to phone him and request a meeting. *Marcus, you're overthinking things. It could be for financial advice? No, doctors don't get paid that much, do they? He had a couple of neurosurgeons and heart specialists as clients, but Rachel and Annabel were just normal doctors. They wouldn't have the sort of money to invest in much.*

Marcus continued to mumble as he drove all the way to Madera Drive. Was Annabel in trouble? Did she need his help again? Was she ill? He passed the short drive in a state of melancholy, until he pulled up and saw Rachel already waiting for him outside the café. Good thing it was a nice day. The little silver tables glinted in the sun, and the bright green umbrellas kept a little shade over the patrons. Getting out of the car, he waved and shouted, 'Hi, Rachel.'

'Marcus, I'm so glad to see you.'

Marcus's heart sank. 'What's wrong with Anna? Tell me.'

'Sit down. Do you want a coffee? My treat,' Rachel offered.

'Not yet. Besides, I should buy you one after being so rude the other night. Just tell me what's wrong.' Marcus had an ominous feeling about this meeting. A cold shiver ran down his spine, and the hairs on the back of his neck stood on end.

Why was Rachel smiling? It wasn't nice to smile if something was wrong. 'Marcus, oh forget about that and just sit down. There's nothing wrong. Well, not exactly,' Rachel admitted.

He didn't like the not exactly part.

'Go on. I'm waiting.' He bounced his heel up and down beneath the table.

'Annabel is ill as such, but it will pass soon enough.'

Marcus reached for Rachel's hand. 'What do you mean she is sick? How sick? I mean, is she going to be all right?'

'Marcus, calm down.' Rachel smiled. It was just as she suspected. Marcus was totally and utterly in love with her best friend. 'Before I tell you, can you answer me something honestly?'

'Of course.'

'Have you started seeing your ex again?' Rachel watched him intently.

'Heavens no, Rachel. I had to find her to tell her about — ' But Marcus couldn't say it; he presumed Rachel would know all about it anyway, and there was no need to speak about it further. His hand automatically touched his pocket. He still carried Emily's picture with him. 'Besides, it had been all Anna's bright idea, and then she just walked away.'

'I know. That's what I thought,' she said, nodding her agreement.

Marcus could see Rachel was hesitating. 'Just tell me. It can't be that bad, can it?' He braced himself for whatever it was.

'Annabel has morning sickness.'

He had no idea what Rachel was talking about. *Everyone gets ill at one time or another.* Then it hit him. 'But that would mean . . . that would mean . . . ' He stumbled over his words.

'Yes, Marcus, it does.' Rachel smiled at him.

He felt his heart fill. 'I'm pregnant? Seriously? I mean, she's pregnant. No, she can't be. How did she get pregnant?'

'Do you really need me to explain the birds and the bees to you, Marcus?

Then he thought for a moment. 'Is it mine?' What a stupid-ass question. *Of course it isn't yours. You've not seen her for a few weeks.*

'Of course it is. My boyfriend

examined her and said ten weeks. You do the math.'

'Where is she?' Marcus stood. All he needed was to know where to find her.

'She's at home, Marcus.' It was all Rachel said to him, but he didn't need to hear any more.

'Listen, Marcus, you two need to sit down and really talk. I know she's hurting, and I don't want to see her like this anymore.' Rachel's tone carried a warning.

'But she left me, said to go and see Josie. I don't know what possessed her to think I would take Josie back.'

'I don't know, but you're having a baby, and I am definitely not the one you should be talking to.'

Marcus was too overjoyed to pay much attention. Could Rachel be right? Could Anna be pregnant? But what if he lost them like he lost Emily? No, no, nothing could happen to Anna or his child. He loved Anna so much. It was time he told her instead of keeping his love a secret as he had for all these years.

'Thank you. Thank you.' He dashed back to his car. 'Bye,' he shouted quickly over his shoulder. Annabel was pregnant, and it was his. Why hadn't she told him?

It took him less than ten minutes to get to Annabel's house. He hadn't exactly obeyed the speed limits to get there, but if he had been stopped, he would have just said it was an emergency and hoped he would get away with it. He should have stopped off and got Annabel some flowers and chocolates or teddy bears and balloons. Isn't that what expectant fathers give to the mother of their child? He had been too excited to even consider such a trivial thing.

Cautiously, Marcus went up to the bright red front door. Did Emily mind that he was going to be a dad again? What if she hated the idea? His soul was drowning as a tidal wave of guilt washed over him. Grabbing the lion's-head doorknocker, he knocked several times.

Long torturous minutes passed, and no one came to the door. Was she in trouble? Wasn't she in? The thoughts ran through his head like a bullet train. Just as he was about to give up, the door opened slightly.

'Marcus?'

Annabel stood there in a dressing gown, looking like she had done ten rounds with a garden hedge. 'Can I come in?' he asked cautiously.

'I guess.' Annabel opened the door wider for him so he could enter her messy domain.

Marcus looked around, there seemed to be stuff everywhere, not at all like his empty shell of a home. 'Just like the flat then.'

'I guess. Marcus, I don't mean to be rude, but what are you doing here?'

'I've seen your friend,' he blurted out. 'I know about the baby, Annabel.'

'Good news sure travels fast.' Annabel was incensed. 'I thought friends were meant to be trusted.'

'Sweets, she only told me because she

cares.' Marcus ran his hand down her arm.

'Look, I'm not going to interrupt yours and Josie's life.' Annabel still held onto the open door. 'Please, just go.'

She really did think that he had taken Josie back. This had to be sorted out before it was too late. Annabel's eyes were puffy and red. He could see she had been crying.

'No, I'm not going anywhere until you talk to me.'

Marcus pushed the door closed, and Annabel didn't have the strength to stop him. He was shocked at the paleness of her face, her skin lacked the glow that many people had when they were pregnant. Had she even eaten anything? Maybe he should have brought her something to eat, but he hadn't thought things through properly. Maybe he should leave and come back with food? If he left would she let him back into the house?

'Marcus.'

'Look, Anna, you need to sit down.'

'I'm pregnant, that's all.' But she allowed him to steer her into the front room.

Marcus sat her gently on the sofa, taking a seat beside her. 'Listen, babe. I didn't think that after Emily died, I could feel so alive again.'

Annabel stared at the floor. She wouldn't look at him, but he could tell she was hurting just as much as he was. He'd hated hearing her say good-bye the first time, but he wouldn't survive her saying it again.

'You brought me back.'

'How have I done that? You're with Josie. Look, you can see our baby; I won't stop you.' She paused. 'Just go, please. I've had enough.' Annabel moved to the comer of the sofa, putting distance between them.

'No, I will go once you have listened to me.'

'There's nothing to say. I'm sorry you lost your daughter, and it was wrong of me not to be there to talk to.' She looked out the window. 'You have your wife back. You will be happy again.'

'Ex-wife,' he interjected. 'I don't want to be with anyone but you. I said *you* brought me back and you have.'

'I don't understand. I — '

Marcus interrupted her. 'You did that. The way you fought to keep the hospital ward open. You helped all those people at the service station.'

'I didn't — '

'Yes, you did,' Marcus replied sternly. 'You took charge whilst everyone else stood and looked on.'

'Marcus, I did my job. That's all, just my job.'

He was so proud of what she had done, how she had taken care of everyone including him. Annabel had never seen herself clearly, and this was no exception, but he was determined to make her change her mind about herself.

'You made me see that, although I had lost something precious, my life wasn't over. I could live again, love again, and be happy. I imagine what she would say — 'Daddy, don't be sad anymore.' She said that all the time if I ever looked sad or upset about work. When I packed her toys away, I could hear her voice telling me everything would be okay.' He reached for her, but Annabel moved away. 'I know I must sound like I'm crazy, but I'm not. If I need her, she is here in my head, my heart, in everything I do, and I want to make her so proud of her daddy.'

'Marcus, she would be proud of you. I wasn't the only one to help all those people. You did too and helped raise all that money.'

Marcus looked shocked. 'You knew about the sponsorship money.'

Annabel touched his face. 'Of course, I realized when you told me what your daughter had — I knew.'

'I wasn't sure if I should tell you. I hated to think that you considered our relationship payback for the money. No matter what I did, you were still so unsure of me, and I had to gain your trust without you feeling obligated.'

Marcus was worried he was losing the battle. He wanted so much for Annabel to understand. Now was the perfect time to reveal the drawing he had planned to show her.

'Will this change your mind?' Marcus pulled a piece of paper out of his pocket and handed it to her. 'I found it by the Christmas tree.'

Confusion flashed on Annabel's face. 'Who on earth would have a Christmas tree up in July?'

'Me, at the house,' he replied sheepishly. 'I couldn't face taking it down, whilst all her presents lay underneath. That's why I live in a hotel. The house is too empty.'

Annabel unfolded Emily's drawing of a house and a family. A drawing of so much hope, so much love, etched onto the paper in bright colors. 'Emily.' It wasn't a question more a statement.

'She wanted a mum and a little sister. On the front of the envelope, she had written *To Santa.*'

'You and Josie could have more

children,' she replied.

Marcus grabbed her shoulders. 'There is no me and Josie! Aren't you listening to anything I am saying?' Marcus stood and paced around the room. 'I went to tell her about Emily, just like you told me to.' He slammed his hand down on the fireplace. 'She wasn't bothered. Didn't care that my little girl was gone.' The grief that Marcus felt poured out of him. He had tried so hard to bottle it all up, hide it away in his dungeon of self-pity. He sat back down again right up against her. She shuddered, his beautiful Anna. 'So you see, I was sent on a fool's journey. I know it was only right she should know, but — '

'I thought . . . I thought I was just another — ' Annabel tripped over her words. 'It seemed so right, and then you told me. Grief makes people do stupid things.'

Marcus's heart broke to see Anna so upset, so small. 'Well, grief made this biker almost lose the best thing to ever happen to him.

'But you got your bike back.'

Marcus laughed heartily; this woman was going to drive him crazy. She was always so insecure and unsure of herself. 'One day, sweets, you will see yourself clearly, and I intend to make sure you do.'

'I love you, but you didn't — '

'Oh, sweets, I love you. I have always loved you.'

He felt Annabel wrap her arms around him. She held him close, but it felt all wrong. He should be holding her. Marcus removed her arms from around his neck and pulled her into his embrace. He watched how Anna curled up on the sofa with her head against his chest.

'You've always loved me?'

He stroked her back. 'Yes, I even loved you that summer, except I was too stupid and immature to do anything about it. Then you walked away from me, and I had no idea why.'

'I thought you had walked away.'

'No, I wouldn't do that to you. I

admit I had done that in the past with other people, but you have always been special.'

'I just didn't want you to think you made a mistake.'

'You were never a mistake.' To prove his point, he lifted Annabel toward him, brushing his lips against hers, then roughly claiming her. They kissed hungrily; all the passion and all the heartache they had experienced came out in their kiss. When they eventually came up for air, Marcus needed to tell her what he had found out about the hospital fraud.

'When I came home, I met Mr. Underwood and told him everything I had found out about the hospital funds.'

'What did he say?'

'Well, to be honest, he didn't seem that shocked. He seemed to have an idea something was going on. Mr. Wild had been taking funds from the hospital, putting your ward at risk of closure.'

'So it was Mr. Wild. Has he been arrested?'

'Not just him, sweets, but, Mrs. Higginbottom as well.'

Annabel raised her head to look at him briefly. 'Tell me you are joking?'

'I wish I was. They were in it together, as on company accounts you need two signatures.'

Annabel stared at him, her mouth open slightly.

'That way one partner is not committing fraud, but — '

'I don't understand?'

'I will explain another day; right now I have more important things to think about.'

'What would that be?' she purred.

'Making love to you would be a good start.'

'I like that idea. I'm sorry. I thought you would get back with Josie.'

'There will never be a me and Josie again,' he replied softly. 'Haven't you figured it out yet? And besides, I just told you.'

'Maybe I need — '

'To hear it again? I love you and only you.'

'I thought — '

Marcus held her tight. 'I know what you thought.' When he lifted her chin so she looked at him, her eyes brimmed with unshed tears. 'I have only ever loved one person other than Emily, and she decided to walk out on me before I had a chance to tell her.'

'Who was that?'

'I will give you one guess.'

The tears she was holding back spilled. 'I love you, so much it hurts.'

'Oh, Annabel.' He pulled her into his arms, her body wracked with sobs. He stroked her head and back as he held her tightly to him. They had wasted so much time when they could have been happy. He wiped her tears away gently with his fingers before crushing his mouth against hers. The sparkle he thought had extinguished was still there hidden behind all the pain and hurt and grew as he repeated, 'I love you,' over and over.

'I never want to be without you. Emily was telling me she wanted a sister and a new mum, and you would have been perfect.' Everything was falling into place. 'We can be a family.' He placed his hand on her stomach.

★ ★ ★

Annabel never thought she would feel such happiness again, and she wasn't going to throw this chance away.

'You still want me?' Her voice shook from her crying.

'Of course I want you. Who could not?' He kissed her head. 'Marry me, Anna?'

'Oh, Marcus, I don't know what to say.'

'Yes would be a good idea.' He chuckled. 'I want to spend the rest of my life making you happy.'

'Yes, oh, Marcus, yes.' Annabel kissed him back, a slow lingering kiss full of so much promise and hope; they would have so much to look forward to. A whole new life to share. Everything that had happened had been worth it. Annabel had everything she had ever dreamed of and so much more. She wondered when the right time would be to tell Marcus the ultrasound showed twins!